WAIT

F⊙R

IT

I0527633

By A.L. Glennon

Ink Smith Publishing

www.ink-smith.com

To Jason.

One lifetime together doesn't seem like enough.

ISBN: 978-1-947578-28-9

Ink Smith Publishing
P.O. Box 361
Lakehurst, NJ 08733

Chapter 1

Martin had always been the kind of no-nonsense, down-to-Earth guy who kept both feet planted firmly on the ground. Which is why he found it so terribly disorienting to suddenly realize he was hurtling head-over-heels through space at a sickening rate of speed. A cold, violent wind tried to blow Martin right out of his skin, and colors he couldn't even name swirled around him in a nauseating blur.

Even more upsetting was the strange squeezing sensation that arrested his forward momentum. It was as if Martin's entire being had suddenly slammed into an invisible wall and was now striving for two-dimensionality. The flattening feeling was followed by a head-first dive through a thick, plasma-like substance that made Martin feel three-dimensional once more. He made a clumsy landing on what seemed to be an industrial-strength, low-nap carpet in the hallway of an office building.

Martin lay on the crummy carpet for a minute, catching his breath and gingerly flexing his extremities to ascertain whether he'd been hurt during his adventure.

When he couldn't find anything wrong with himself, he sat up carefully and looked around. He was definitely in some kind of professional-building hallway, though he didn't recognize it. A bank of elevators stood to his right. A frosted-glass door marked RECEPTION AND WAITING lay directly in front of him at the end of the short corridor. The other two walls were solid, covered in sleek gray paneling that was probably supposed to look chic and contemporary. Martin thought it looked cheap and uninspired.

Martin tried to remember how he'd gotten to the building. Did he have some kind of an appointment to keep there? One minute he'd been...well, he couldn't exactly recall...and the next minute he'd been flying through the air, landing awkwardly in the gray hallway.

Martin stood up carefully, still in shock that he was uninjured. He patted his pockets, feeling for his phone. When he didn't find it, he figured he must have lost it in his fall. Or in being flattened into two dimensions. Or in hurtling through the air. Whatever. In any case, it was missing, and Martin felt positively marooned without it.

A filtered glow came through the glass of the RECEPTION AND WAITING door, and Martin headed toward it. A receptionist might be able to shed some light on what he was doing there, and she'd probably be happy to let him use the office phone. Maybe she'd even fetch him a cup of coffee. He felt like he could use a little kick of caffeine to get him through what was turning into a very trying afternoon. Yes, Martin could use a nice reception, so he pushed open the door to RECEPTION AND WAITING.

The reception area was decorated very much like the hallway, done up in muted grays, more glass, and metallics. Wall sconces with frosted-glass shades sent soothing beams of light upward to bounce off the ceiling and bathe the room in a pleasant white glow.

Martin approached a glass reception counter and was thrilled to see both a pretty young receptionist and a small coffee maker installed there. He couldn't decide which one to take advantage of first.

"Name?" the receptionist asked, making Martin's decision for him. She was beautiful, with honey-colored highlights in her dark hair, smooth caramel skin, and dark chocolate eyes. Hmmm. Martin had always been slightly hypoglycemic. Maybe he was having some kind of an episode. Maybe he needed a little sugar.

Whether or not she was a hallucination, the receptionist was still staring at him, waiting for an answer.

"Uh, my name?" Martin said, eyeing the coffee maker. "The thing is, I don't think I have an appointment."

"No," the receptionist said. "You don't. I was just trying to be polite. I actually have your paperwork right here. It just came through. Go ahead." She waved a hand toward the coffee maker. "Help yourself."

"Oh. Uh. Thanks," Martin said. The machine was unlike any he'd used before. He studied it intently before finally slipping a foam cup underneath a nozzle and pushing a blinking green button. "Thanks a lot," he said as steaming brown liquid filled his cup.

"Here are some forms," the receptionist said, passing a clipboard and pen over the glass countertop. "And a manual, of course."

"Sorry, what?" Martin said. "I actually can't stay. I was just wondering if I could use your phone?"

The receptionist stared at Martin. "No," she said.

Martin paused, his coffee cup halfway to his lips. "No?"

"No," she repeated and smiled. "Here." She thrust the forms and the manual at him again. "Please take these and have a seat over there." She pointed to a walled-off area with a glass door that said WAITING on it.

"Waiting?" Martin said, taking the forms and the book, just to be polite. "But what am I waiting for?"

"Because you don't have an appointment," the receptionist said. "Excuse me." She stood up, grabbed some folders from her desk, and disappeared into a back room.

Martin decided he'd had enough. He wasn't sure what had happened to him, but he knew he didn't need to wait around in an office suite anymore. He turned back the way he'd come, planning to go back to the bank of elevators in the hallway and find an exit to the street. But the glass RECEPTION AND WAITING door he'd come through wasn't where he remembered it. In fact, it wasn't anywhere at all, which Martin found extremely disconcerting. He brought his coffee cup up to his lips and took a sip. The liquid inside was warm, but flavorless. Was every little thing going to be a huge disappointment today?

Martin glanced down at the forms and the little book in his other hand, looking for a clue about where he'd landed and how he might get home. He read the title of the manual once, then he read it again. Then, he took another sip of his crappy office-brewed coffee and read it a third time, just to be sure he hadn't misread it the first two. It said, in unmistakable black Arial type on a blank white field, *Soul Reassignment Procedures and Policies: A Manual*.

Huh, Martin thought.

He took another sip of his coffee. His head was starting to spin a little bit. He decided to take the receptionist's advice and have a seat in the waiting area after all. He moved toward the glass WAITING door on leaden feet. Martin pushed it open, stumbled through, and heard the door seal itself shut behind him with a suction-y sound.

Huh, he thought again. He'd never felt so unbrilliant. Martin took another sip of the piss-warm water in his foam cup and collapsed into a gray upholstered chair with a well-worn seat. It appeared to have seen a lot of waiting in its time. Martin looked around. The waiting-room walls were windowless and plain. No posters, no hotel-style artwork. There wasn't so much as a potted plant to break up the monotony of the plain gray wallpaper and shabby chairs.

Martin placed his clipboard and the bizarrely titled manual in his lap and looked them over with a frown. The manual wasn't thick, but it was filled with pages and pages of uninterrupted, single-spaced black type. The clipboard had several forms attached to it. The top one was pre-printed with Martin's name and birthdate, which he found odd since, as he and the receptionist had both noted, he hadn't made any kind of appointment. Even odder, the forms all said, "Soul Reassignment Office" across the top, which gave Martin a very nervous feeling right in the middle of his gut. Even so, the straight-A student in him wanted to fill in as many correct answers as he could before someone came around to collect his paperwork. So, he uncapped the pen (which also bore the same unsettling Soul Reassignment Office name) and went to work.

Question 1: How did you leave your last assignment?
    A. Voluntarily
    B. Involuntarily

Uh. Martin blinked at the words, hoping they'd reform themselves into a question that made more sense. When they didn't, he employed an age-old test-taking technique he'd learned in grade school: When stumped by one question, move on to the next.

Question 2: The purpose of your last life was:
A. Fulfilled
B. Partially Fulfilled
C. Mostly Unfulfilled
D. Completely Unfulfilled

What the…?

Martin looked up from the paper. Another, less scrupulous, test-taking strategy he knew was to look around the room at what people nearby were writing on their papers. Unfortunately, the only other people in the waiting area were sitting across the way from Martin. They sat next to each other, but didn't seem to be acknowledging each other's presence. Their clipboards were set aside, their forms presumably completed.

One of them, a lanky boy wearing dirty, dark skinny jeans and a V-necked black t-shirt, sat slumped in his chair. His head rested against the dull gray wall, his wild, curly brown hair splayed out behind him. He crossed one ankle over the other knee and jiggled a black-boot-clad foot up and down frantically, but no other part of him moved. His heavy-lidded eyes didn't even seem to be blinking.

Next to him, a girl in some kind of medieval dress looked more than a little bored and pissed off. Martin's eyes were drawn first to her wine-red corset top, which showed off quite a bit of cleavage, then he took in her blousy, muslin sleeves adorned with gold arm garters and a full red skirt that billowed around the legs of her chair. Martin's

eyes finally made their way up to the girl's face and took in
the strange gold circlet she wore around her head and the
big red jewel that dangled between her eyes. She had been
picking at her cuticles, but she must have felt Martin
gawking because she glanced up at him and twisted her
heavily made-up face into a sneer.

"What are you looking at?" she snapped.

"Nothing," Martin answered quickly. He felt
underdressed in his plain khaki pants, sneakers, and hooded
Honor Society sweatshirt.

He looked back down at his paperwork and pretended
to contemplate the bizarre questions in front of him. He'd
been planning to ask the girl what she got for number one,
but chickened out. Girls had always intimidated Martin,
especially the kinds of girls who wore crowns and lots of
makeup. Not to mention corset tops.

The boy across the room sat up straighter, looking more
alert. He had wild eyes to match his wild hair and he fixed
them on Martin, who stopped pretending he might know
any of the answers to the questions on his forms and
nervously met his gaze.

"Well, well, well," the boy said, unfolding his unusually
long and lean body from the waiting-room chair and taking
a few steps toward Martin. "What do we have here?" He
seemed to have just taken notice of Martin.

Martin didn't like the way the other boy towered over
him. Tall people were always doing that, he thought,
lording their extra inches over those of—oh, how Martin
hated this word—*average* height. Martin sat up a little
straighter in his chair before he spoke.

"Excuse me?" Martin said.

"You a virgin?" the boy asked him.

"I beg your pardon!" Martin huffed self-righteously, trying not to let his cheeks redden.

"You don't have to answer me," the boy said, smiling a crazy, crooked smile. "I can see that you are."

"Whatever," Martin said, and looked toward the door to the hallway. He decided he'd had enough of the crazy forms and didn't really want to deal with a crazy boy, too. In fact, Martin quite wanted to leave.

"There's no exit," the boy said, and laughed. "There's only one way out of the building for people like us, and you can't get through on your own."

"Mmm-hmm. I understand," Martin said placatingly, even though he didn't understand anything at all. The wildness of the strange boy's hair compelled Martin to run a hand through his own very tame and conservatively short brown mop. He hated how clueless and out of control he felt. Martin thumbed through the book the receptionist had handed him, looking for answers or advice and trying to forget about the unfairly tall boy in front of him. The guy was clearly nuts, and lunatics tended to put Martin on edge. Almost as much as heavily made-up girls in crowns and corset tops.

"OK, newbie. Fine. Ignore me. Look for answers in your precious manual. But you won't find any. You're screwed. Trust me. I've done this a million times already. You're screwed, I'm screwed, she's screwed, and there's no way out."

"What do you mean we're screwed?" the girl in the centuries-old dress said. "I thought we just had to wait here!"

"Yes," the crazy-eyed kid replied. "And what do you think we're waiting for?"

"Soul reassignment?" the girl answered, somewhat uncertain.

"Exactly," the boy said. "Another go-round on good old planet Earth. It's like being on a hamster wheel! We just got off, and they're going to throw us right back on. Look!" The boy pointed through the glass door of the reception area. A smiling young man in a suit and tie was being led through the hallway by a pretty, skirt-suited woman. She swiped some kind of access card over a black square on the wall opposite the waiting room and a rectangle began to draw itself there in bright white light. Soon, the rectangle swung inward, just like a door, revealing a huge swath of light. Martin blinked and shielded his eyes with one hand. The woman hugged the young man fondly. He smiled, and headed through the opening. Then, the door shut slowly behind him as the woman walked away. In a matter of seconds, it was like the door had never existed at all.

"What the…?" Martin mumbled.

"That's what I'm trying to tell you, Purgatory Virgin. They're sending us all back. We have to do it all over again. Shit our pants, learn to walk, get bullied on the playground. We have to start from scratch. And for what? It's all so fucking pointless."

The boy flopped down into the chair next to Martin, who instinctively leaned away from him. The boy slumped against the wall again.

"I'm Zeke, by the way," the boy said. "Ezekiel Zabar. At least I was, for a little while. Who knows what piece-of-shit moniker they'll give me in my next life."

"Oh. Uh. I'm Martin," Martin said. "Pleased to meet you."

Zeke smirked. "Likewise, I'm sure," he said, his tone making it clear that he was mocking Martin's attempt at manners.

"So," Martin said. "Let me get this straight. We're…?"

"Dead." Zeke sighed. "Yeah."

"Don't say that!" the girl sitting across from them said.

Zeke snorted. "Deceased. Gone. Departed. Whatever."

"I don't feel dead," Martin said.

"Well, you are," Zeke assured him.

"That just doesn't make sense, though," Martin insisted. "I mean, dying really isn't something I would do. I hope you won't take offense if I suggest that this is all just a bizarre dream."

The girl laughed a short, flat laugh.

"Tell me," Zeke said. "Do they often hand out paperwork in your dreams?" He tapped Martin's clipboard with his foot.

"Well, no," Martin said.

"And how did you get here?" Zeke asked.

"I flew," Martin mumbled. "I landed in the hallway, I came inside, and then the exit just…disappeared."

Zeke nodded knowingly.

"Those are all things that could happen in a dream."

"OK, then," Zeke said. "What were you doing right before you started 'dreaming'?"

Martin tried hard to remember. "Well, I was….Let me think. It was just an average afternoon…I went to— Oh!" Martin suddenly felt woozy.

Zeke smirked triumphantly.

10

Martin was quiet for a minute. Then, he cleared his throat and sat up. "So, we died—I died!— and…?" Martin was still hoping none of this was actually happening, but, just in case it was, he wanted to get all the facts.

"And we're waiting for our soul's next assignment," Zeke said. "Obviously."

"Obviously," Martin said even though nothing at all seemed obvious to him. "And you've done this before?"

"Yup."

"A bunch?"

"Yup."

"May I ask why?" Martin ventured.

"You may," Zeke said.

Martin waited. Then he got it. "OK," he said. "Why?"

"I thought you'd never ask," Zeke said, grinning with a mouth full of crooked teeth that made Martin recoil a little. He ran his tongue fondly along the front of his own perfect dentition, his teeth having been painstakingly straightened by years in braces.

"Because life on Earth sucks ass," Zeke told Martin. "I can only stand it for so long, and I never last long enough to fulfill my purpose there, so they keep sending me back."

"You mean…?"

"Suicide."

"Wow."

"Fifty-nine times."

"Oh."

"Yeah," Zeke said. "Oh." He sighed. "The worst part is that I remember all fifty-nine times."

"What?"

"Yeah," Zeke said. "I'm not supposed to. Nobody else does, right? But I remember everything about every life they've forced me to live. It's been driving me what some people on Earth call crazy, actually."

"You are crazy," the girl said, still frowning down at her poor, shredded cuticles. "You keep going to Earth just to kill yourself before you fulfill your purpose for being there? That's nuts. They say the definition of insanity is doing the same thing over and over again and expecting different results. If you were even a little bit sane, you'd just suck it up for, like, one lifetime, and move on."

"Well, what the fuck do you know about it?" Zeke shouted. "You're a freaking Purgatory Virgin, too! You know what? All those people they call crazy down on Earth? They're the only truly sane ones. They *know*, man! They're the only ones who really know what's going on. They remember everything, just like I do. They know that it's all bullshit, that they're going to have to come back and do it all over and over again. That knowledge is enough to drive anyone around the bend."

"Killing yourself is never the answer," Martin said sagely, quoting from a guidance-office poster he'd walked past every day last school year.

"Says you," Zeke said. "I'm just waiting until I can get a tolerable assignment. Then I'll 'suck it up' or whatever. All these lives they've given me have been total duds."

Nobody spoke for a minute, then Martin said. "So, just to recap here, *we're dead*?"

"As doornails."

The girl in the red dress flinched.

"And they're going to…?"

"Reassign our souls to new lives and remind us of our purposes so we can fulfill them and move on to even higher purposes, then higher ones. It's a vicious cycle. Get one assignment right, get an even harder one handed to you. It's complete bullshit."

"Right," Martin said. "So, how long do you think this is all going to take?"

"Well," Zeke said. "Unfortunately for us, we arrived without an appointment."

"So I've heard," Martin said. "But what does that mean?"

"We died too soon," Zeke said. "Unexpectedly. If we'd lived out the courses of our natural lives the way they'd mapped them out for us, they'd have our paperwork in order and a new assignment all ready to go and we'd be in and out of here. But, catch them off guard and the whole staff of the afterlife has to scramble around and make arrangements on the fly."

Another relaxed, smiling pair of well-dressed folks strolled past the waiting area and Martin and Zeke watched as the door of light opened up in the wall. The annoyingly satisfied customer passed through.

"See?" Zeke asked bitterly. "Stick to their plan and there's no wait time." He stood up and pounded on the glass as the light door closed and the staff member who'd opened it started to walk away. "Hey!" Zeke yelled, pounding on the glass again. "We were here first! This is bullshit!"

The staff member ignored him and Zeke sat back down and sighed.

"So, how long does it usually take?" Martin asked. He nodded in the direction of the girl with the circlet on her head. "I mean, it looks like maybe sometimes it can take quite a while…?"

Zeke started laughing so hard his chair shook. Martin couldn't imagine sitting in the waiting area with Zeke for centuries. He'd kill himself. Or, well, no, he guessed he probably wouldn't be able to if it were true that he was already dead. But, whatever. He really didn't want to sit there for hundreds of years with a crazy kid.

Zeke kept laughing and pointing at the girl in the red dress.

"Shut up," she said, angrily. She looked at Martin. "I was on my way to a Renaissance festival, OK?"

"What?" Martin said.

Zeke snorted and wiped some tears from his eyes.

"It's a costume!" the girl said, her eyes flashing.

"Oh!" said Martin, relieved. "I thought. I mean. I dunno. I thought you died like, back in the Middle Ages."

"Dork," the girl said.

"The chick in the role-playing costume is calling someone a dork?" Zeke said, still laughing. "This is too much. Seriously. I'm going to piss myself if you two don't stop it." Zeke stood up and moved toward the glass door.

"Where are you going?" Martin asked.

"To take a piss," Zeke said.

"You can do that here?"

Zeke looked thoughtful for a minute. "Let me see," he said. A big, wet stain started to spread across the front of his pants. "Yes. Apparently, I can piss in Purgatory. It didn't give me any real sense of relief, of course, just like that coffee you're drinking—," Zeke gestured to the half-full foam cup Martin had all but forgotten about. "Is probably completely flavorless. But, at least they let us go through the motions. It's nice to keep up our little Earthly rituals, isn't it?" Zeke didn't wait for an answer. He opened the glass door and headed off down the gray hallway, presumably looking for a completely unnecessary, but mentally reassuring, restroom in which to finish his business and dry his pants.

Zeke left an awkward silence in his wake.

"I'm sorry," Martin finally said.

"For what?" the girl asked.

"For…I dunno? For presuming you were hundreds of years old?"

The girl smiled a resigned little half-smile. "That's OK," she said. "I guess this is kind of a ridiculous outfit to be wearing, especially given the circumstances." There was another short pause and then she said, "Just ignore Zeke, OK? He doesn't have as many answers as he thinks he does."

"OK," said Martin. He racked his brain for something else to say to the strange girl across from him. He was either dreaming or dead and, either way, he figured this was his big chance to be brave and chat up a girl. What was the worst that could happen, right?

"So, waiting around here really sucks, huh?" was the best he could come up with.

"Yeah," she said. "It does."

"They could at least give us some magazines or something to look at, right?" God. Even dead, Martin knew he was totally lame.

"They gave me a book," the girl said, pointing toward her manual, sitting unopened on a side table.

"Me, too," Martin said, picking his up and thumbing through it. "Maybe there's a cryptogram or something," he joked. The girl didn't laugh.

"Oh, wow!" Martin said, letting the book fall open on his lap. "Look at this!" The girl stood up, her skirts swishing, and crossed to where Martin was sitting. Together, they stared at a chapter heading: "Things to Do While You Wait for Reassignment."

"Huh," the girl said.

"Number one," Martin read out loud. "Review this manual." The girl snorted and started fiddling with her cuticles again. Martin read on, if only for the sake of having something to say. "Number two: Wonder where it all went wrong." They both chuckled at that one. "Number three: Lament missed opportunities and list regrets from last Earthly life."

"There," the girl said. "Now that sounds fun. And it could take up a crapload of time."

"OK," Martin said. "You start."

"I regret dying," the girl said. Her voice sounded clipped and her lip trembled a little. Martin was afraid she was going to break down and sob, but she took several deep breaths to steady herself. "I shouldn't be here!" she shouted, her eyes widening as though realizing it for the first time. "I'm not supposed to be here!" She gripped the arms of her chair and breathed in and out.

Martin stared as her corseted bosom heaved, then tore his eyes away and patted her awkwardly on the back. "None of us are supposed to be here," he said. "Right? Something went wrong or we'd be like those other people breezing through that light door in the hallway."

"But it's my own stupid fault," the girl said, still breathing hard. "I made some really shitty choices."

"I'm sorry," Martin said, patting her a little too enthusiastically on the back. With his other hand, he frantically turned pages in the manual. "Maybe there's something else we can do while we wait."

"No," she said. "It's OK. I mean, it is what it is, right?" The girl wiped at her sweat-damp face, smearing some of her makeup onto the sleeve of her Renaissance costume. She sniffled a little and blinked fast. "OK," she finally said, trying to sound perky. "Your turn."

"My turn?"

"Yeah. Missed opportunities? Regrets?"

"Oh," Martin felt himself turn red. "I dunno. I was gonna say something like I was sorry I hadn't kissed Mary Ellen Keibler at homecoming when I had the chance, but that sounds really lame now."

The girl laughed. "Yeah," she said. "It totally does."

Martin thought back on that dance—his sweaty palms, his too-tight necktie. If only he'd known it was his last school dance! He would have...he would have...probably still been too nervous to make his move on Mary Ellen, damn it. Martin sighed heavily and slumped a little in his chair.

They were quiet while the girl sniffled into her voluminous sleeves and Martin tried to think of something to say.

"So," the girl finally said, breaking the silence. "Did you seriously die without ever being kissed?"

"No!" Martin said hotly, his face aflame. "I mean...nah. No. I kissed plenty of people. Just that one got away."

"Oh yeah?" She looked amused.

"Yeah," Martin said. "I made out with, like, everyone at my school." He felt himself blushing all the way to the neckline of his hooded Honor Society sweatshirt.

"OK," the girl said. Then, without warning, she leaned over and pressed her lips against his.

At first, Martin recoiled, appalled at the idea of locking lips with a total stranger. Then he came to his senses and leaned forward and started kissing her back. She tasted like tears and lipstick and…was that mud? Martin reached for her and his hand found her bare shoulder. He pulled her toward him, both of them pressed against the arms of the waiting room chairs between them.

"Hell-fucking-lo!"

They hadn't heard Zeke come in. He stood over them, mouth agape, foam coffee cup steaming in his hand.

Martin and the Renaissance girl sprang apart, the girl wiping her lips on her sleeve, Martin looking the fool with lipstick smeared on the corner of his still-puckered mouth.

The girl's eyes widened and she took another deep breath. "See?" she said. "See what's wrong with me? I'm so impetuous!"

"If by impetuous, you mean slutty, then I'd have to agree," Zeke said, blowing on the hot liquid in his cup that wouldn't, they all knew, taste like coffee when he got around to drinking it.

"There, there," Martin said, putting his arms around the still-panic-stricken girl in red.

"Did I take a wrong turn and end up in Hell?" Zeke asked loudly, looking around with exaggerated confusion. "Get off my girlfriend, newbie!"

Martin stood up and backed away. "Sorry!" he said. "I'm sorry. I— She—! We—! Wait, what?"

"Save it," Zeke said. He took Martin's seat next to the girl and took a sip of his so-called coffee.

Martin sat down across the room. He felt nervous and shaky and excited. He tried to steady himself.

The girl looked soberly between Martin and Zeke. "I'm sorry," she said.

"To whom?" Martin asked. If he sounded a little miffed, fine. He felt like he had every right to be. His first kiss had been stolen from him by a stranger who was going out with someone else.

"To whom?" the girl repeated.

"Yes," Martin said. "To whom are you apologizing?"

"Uh. Both of you?"

"Whatever, babe," Zeke said.

"But, I was your girlfriend," she said. "I shouldn't have done that."

Zeke shrugged. "It only matters for, like, five more minutes anyway. You won't remember me in your next life."

"I can't believe this is your boyfriend!" Martin said. He was feeling really agitated now. He stood up and started pacing back and forth across the small waiting area.

Zeke laughed.

The girl shrugged. "I'm a gamer chick who likes Renaissance festivals and role-playing games," she said a little defensively. "It's not like I was going to get asked out by the prom king."

"I'm not so dead I can't hear you, you know," Zeke said, sounding more amused than offended.

19

"But, still!" Martin shouted, ignoring Zeke and focusing on the corset-clad girl instead. He was starting to pace faster and wave his arms around, something he tended to do when he got upset. "I'm sure you could have done a little bit better for yourself, right? A drama geek, maybe? Or a nice vo-tech type?" He couldn't believe that the first girl he'd ever laid hands on could actually be coupled up with an anti-social lunatic like Zeke Zabar.

"Zeke makes things interesting," the girl said with another shrug. She started picking at her cuticles again.

"Thanks, babe," Zeke said. He reached over and squeezed her knee through the fabric of her long dress.

Just as Martin felt his head preparing to explode, the waiting-room door opened and the pretty lady Martin recognized from the reception area stepped halfway through it.

"Martin Van Assen?" she said.

"Yes," Martin stopped pacing and flapping and tried to recover his composure. "Here. Present."

Zeke snorted into his coffee cup.

"Your paperwork?" the lady said.

"Oh. Uh." Martin felt his face getting hot as he took a few steps toward Zeke and retrieved his clipboard. "I. Uh. I didn't have time to finish."

He hadn't answered a single question. Not handing in an assignment on time was a first for Martin.

"I'm. Um. I'm still working," he said.

The receptionist raised an eyebrow at him. "Alright. Just do your best. If you don't know the answer to something, leave it blank. I'll be back in a little while." She looked around the room, narrowed her eyes a bit, then propped the back of one of the waiting-room chairs against the glass door. "Let's leave this door open, shall we?" she said, looking at each of them in turn and sounding for all the world like a teacher who didn't trust her class enough to slip off to the restroom for a minute.

The trio was quiet as they listened to her walk away.

"So, Van Assen, is it?" Zeke said, laughter trying to sneak into his voice. "Martin Van Assen?"

"Yes." Martin stiffened. "It's Dutch."

"What's the translation?" Zeke asked. "Martin of the Asses?"

"Shut up, Zeke the Freak." Martin was embarrassed as soon as the insult was out of his mouth. His childish words just hung there in the quiet of the waiting room, mocking him.

"Good one, Van AssMan," the girl in red said with an eye roll. One of her cuticles was starting to bleed and she stuck her finger in her mouth.

"Now, now," Zeke said to the girl. "Remember about people in glass houses, Zelda Kozikowski."

"Your name is Zelda Kozikowski?" Martin said.

"So what?" The girl, Zelda, was back on the defensive.

"So nothing," Martin said, backing down. "It's just unusual."

"I'm unusual," she said.

Zeke chuckled.

"Were your parents big fans of Zelda Fitzgerald?" Martin asked.

Zeke laughed. Hard.

A pair of smiling, formally-attired young men approached the wall opposite the waiting area and, with the wave of an access card, the door of light appeared. With the waiting-room door propped open, Martin could hear a gentle, oddly inviting humming sound coming from the portal. The men shook hands.

"Congratulations again," the one with the access card said. "We're all so proud of your work."

"Thank you," the other one said, smiling graciously. "I look forward to this next assignment, sir."

The men nodded at each other, then one of them stepped through the door of light with a satisfying swooshing sound and disappeared. The other walked away as the door became a solid wall again.

"I want to go back," Zelda said softly.

"Not me," Zeke said.

"I can't imagine being reassigned," Martin said, sitting down next to Zelda and sighing. "I hadn't even gotten the hang of being Martin Van Assen yet and now I have to go figure out how to be somebody else?"

"Reassignment's a bitch," Zeke said. "And then you die. Again." He took a noisy sip of his bland coffee.

"I had so much to do," Martin said. "There was college, of course. Career. Family. The academic bowl at the end of the month. Oh my God!" Martin clutched at the Honor Society logo on the front of his sweatshirt. "The regional academic bowl finals! I was supposed to be team captain! They're going to give my spot to Brandon Woo, I just know it."

"Maybe you can do those things in your next life," Zelda suggested kindly. "Except the regional academic bowl thing. That sounds like a one-time opportunity."

Martin groaned and held his head in his hands.

"None of it matters," Zeke said. "That's the thing. Go to college, don't go to college. Win a nerd trophy, don't win a nerd trophy. It doesn't fucking matter. None of it means anything. It all leads right back here."

"It's got to mean something," Martin said. "If it were all meaningless, then it wouldn't matter that we died too soon. We're supposed to do something out there, something that means *something*, even if we don't know what it is."

Zeke shook his head. "Let's just agree to disagree about that for now since we have to sit here together for God only knows how long."

"Really," Zelda said. "This is taking forever."

"Forever. One nanosecond. It's all the same here." Zeke drained his coffee cup and let out a fake sigh of satisfaction that irritated Martin to no end. "Ah," he said. "Nothing like a good cup o' joe."

"Are you sure we're not in Hell?" Martin asked. He didn't care if he sounded extremely cranky. "This feels like it might be Hell."

"Yup," Zeke said. "I'm positive."

"How do you know?" Zelda asked.

"The pens," Zeke said, pointing to Martin's pen, which still sat on top of his untouched paperwork on the table. "If we were in Hell, I'm pretty sure the pens would all say, 'Property of Satan,' instead of 'Soul Reassignment Office.'"

Chapter 2

Smiling, happy people continued to parade past the waiting room and cheerfully disappear through the door of light while Martin, Zeke, and Zelda watched and pouted. Nobody came back to collect any paperwork. Nobody even seemed to remember that they were sitting there, waiting.

Zeke stood up and started pacing. He flung his arms out wide and loosened up his shoulders. He seemed to be taking up way more than his fair share of the small waiting room.

"What are you doing?" Martin said, annoyed. "Sit down."

"I'm stretching out my dick," Zeke said. "Don't you have one of those, Van AssMan?"

Martin sighed a huffy little sigh and looked out the door as another good soul went off into the world to live a rich and purposeful life.

"I'm going back," Zelda said, sounding resolute.

"Of course you are," Zeke said, shifting his weight from foot to foot and cracking his long neck. "That's why we're here."

"No," Zelda said. "I mean I'm going back as myself."

"You can't," Zeke told her.

"Fuck you, Zeke," she said. "You're not calling the shots anymore."

"Look, guys," Martin said. "Don't fight. Let's just all chill out, OK?"

"No, Van AssMan," Zelda said. "I won't chill out. You don't make decisions for me, either. You got that? I'm going back. Now. As Zelda Kozikowski."

"What for?" Zeke asked. "Zelda's dead. She's gone. She's no longer relevant down on Planet Earth."

"She's not gone!" Zelda yelled. "She's right here. I'm right here! And I'm relevant. And I don't want to disappear. I don't want to be scratched out and replaced with someone else."

"Aw," Zeke said. "You'll still be you, Zel. Just a different version of you. Maybe even a better version. One that doesn't remember being Zelda Kozikowski in the slightest."

"I don't want to be a better version of me," Zelda said. "I don't feel like I'm done being *this* version!"

"I know what you mean," Martin said. "Like, it's not just the academic bowl. It's everything. The Christmas presents I didn't buy, the screenplay I never got around to writing, the graduation speech I had always seen myself giving."

"Shut up, Van AssMan," Zeke said. "Nobody would have cared about your speech. They wouldn't even have been paying attention. They would have been thinking about how hot they were in their polyester gowns or how much play they were going to get at the after-party and nobody would have heard a word. Someone else can give the speech. That Woo guy. He can do it. And the world will spin on just the same. I'm telling you, stop worrying about stupid, trivial crap. Nothing from your past life matters!"

"Well, it matters to me," Martin said. "And have either of you even thought about your families?"

"No," Zeke said.

"Yes," Zelda answered quietly at the same exact moment.

"Well, I have!" Martin said. "My parents must be beside themselves with grief."

"You flatter yourself," Zeke said, beginning to crack every one of his knuckles in turn.

"I want to see them," Zelda said. "My parents, my sister. I want to make sure my family is alright without me."

"They are," Zeke said. "Or not. Whatever. There's nothing you can do about it if they're not, so why even bother to worry about it? It's not your problem. Nothing back on Earth is your problem anymore. And any minute now, you're going to have a whole lifetime of brand-freaking-new problems to sort out, so why don't you two just chill out and enjoy the rest of our stay here in no man's land?"

"Hang on," Zelda said. "Someone's coming."

Martin briefly thought of the paperwork he had continued to neglect and felt the now-familiar I-forgot-my-homework nervousness overtake him. To his great relief, though, it wasn't the receptionist coming down the hallway, but another happily reassigned soul who'd apparently arrived right on schedule and bypassed the agonizing waiting process.

"Smug bastard," Zeke mumbled. Zelda swatted at him and moved toward the door to watch as the portal opened.

The reassigned boy hugged the woman who was escorting him. She smiled and said something into his ear that made him smile and nod, then she waved her card in front of the black rectangle in the wall and the light door began to open. She hugged her young charge again, briefly, and he disappeared into the blinding white light as his escort turned her back and started off down the hall.

Zelda moved a little closer to the door and, much to Martin's fascination, reached up her skirt. She pulled something from beneath her dress and flung it in the direction of the portal. The three of them watched, wide-eyed, as it wedged itself in the closing door, leaving a thin beam of light visible.

"Holy shit!" Martin said. "You brought a knife?"

"It's a dagger," Zelda said. "Rubber. You know. For the Renaissance festival."

"Of course," Martin said. He'd never been to a Renaissance festival and he was getting the impression from Zelda that, aside from the corseted bosoms, he might not enjoy them very much.

The three souls without appointments looked up and down the gray hallway.

"I'm going," Zelda said. "Are you coming?" She was looking right at Martin.

"Uhm, well, I don't…" Martin had never broken a rule in his life.

"It's now or never," Zelda said, heading out of the waiting area. "And I'm going now."

"I'm coming," Martin said quickly. He had never liked being left behind. Besides, where had following the rules gotten him? Maybe it was time to reinvent himself as a rebel.

"What the hell?" Zeke said, even though nobody formally invited him along. "I'm coming, too. I wouldn't miss how fucked up this is going to be for the whole world."

The three of them moved quickly and quietly across the hallway. When they got to the portal, it was humming loudly, calling to them, and the energy coming through it was almost palpable, thrumming like a good bass line. Zelda pushed the door open with one hand, bent down and retrieved her prop dagger with the other. Then, she stepped through and Martin and Zeke followed.

Chapter 3

Returning to Earth wasn't exactly like flying, nor was it the kind of out-of-control, hurtling-through-space feeling Martin had experienced on his way to the Soul Reassignment Office. It was more like slow-motion skydiving or, at least, what a yellow-bellied, slightly acrophobic guy like Martin imagined skydiving would have been like if he'd ever had the nerve to try it when he was alive. The sensation was not entirely unpleasant.

Zelda slowly drifted to Earth in front of him, and Martin was keenly aware of Zeke right on his heels. The psychopath kept yelling out, "Woo hoo!" and "Wheeeeee!" as if he were on some kind of amusement park thrill ride instead of the journey of a lifetime. It seriously irked Martin. Personally, he felt like the occasion called for some modicum of solemnity.

Zelda landed gracefully on some flat rocks near a large body of water, her skirt floating around her legs and, as the ground drew closer, Martin tried to imitate her easy landing. He failed spectacularly, of course. As the rocks loomed in front of him, he became unreasonably nervous and started flailing his arms, causing him to stumble right into Zelda, who'd been gazing out serenely over the water and shot him a look of annoyance. Zeke plowed into both of them with a loud, "Yee ha!" Martin supposed they were all destined to ruin this adventure for each other and sighed in resignation.

"It's beautiful," Zelda whispered, vaguely awestruck. "I forgot how divinely beautiful the Earth is."

"It's just rocks," said Zeke. "And water. Don't go getting all dramatic on us, OK, Zel? The last thing we need right now is unnecessary drama."

"Well, it is quite pretty," Martin said. He was a born diplomat and still hadn't forgotten that kiss back in the waiting room. "I can definitely see where being… departed…can give one a fresh perspective."

Zeke rolled his eyes. "Whatever, Van AssMan. Do you know you're floating?"

"What?" Martin looked around himself.

"Hovering, actually, I guess," Zeke corrected himself. "We all are. Look! Our feet don't touch the ground! We're, like, flying. Now, that's a thing of beauty!" Zeke took a few step-like motions from side to side and, sure enough, he was gliding more than he was walking.

Martin looked down at his own feet in horror. He, too, was floating an inch above the rocks. "This is crazy!" Martin breathed heavily. He felt very insecure without solid ground beneath his feet. He wanted to grab his companions' arms to steady himself, but refrained.

Zelda seemed less impressed by Zeke's observation as she bobbed in the air beside him. "We're ghosts," she said. "What did you expect?"

"Do I look solid?" Martin asked, panic rising in his chest. He looked down at his rumpled khakis. "Zelda, do I look solid to you?" For some reason, Martin did not want to be transparent.

Zelda looked at him intently. "More or less," she said. "Like, I'm aware of the rocks and Zeke behind you, but you mostly block them out."

"Holy crap!" Martin said, holding his hand up to his face and squinting to see the water through it. "I feel so…insubstantial!"

"Don't worry," Zeke said. "You still look as dorky as ever in your brainiac society sweatshirt." He bent down to pick up a rock, but couldn't. "Damn," he said. He pantomimed skipping a rock out over the water's surface, nodded his head as if he were following it: one, two, three, four imaginary skips before he pretended to let it sink. "So, we're floating, we're not quite opaque, and we can't touch shit. I didn't think it was possible, but this might just suck even more than sitting in that waiting area. See, guys? I told you: Earth just fucking sucks!"

"Nobody made you come," Zelda said. She shivered, though Martin noticed that he couldn't feel anything in terms of temperature at all. Was it hot out? Cold? Was there a breeze? He had no idea, and Martin really hated not knowing things. He wouldn't have said it out loud, but he silently agreed with Zeke that they might not have improved their situations by sneaking through the portal.

"Well, I came," Zeke said. "So, what do we do now?"

"Hang on a minute," Martin said. "Let me consult the manual."

"You brought the manual?" Zeke said. "Unbelievable. We're making an unprecedented run for it across unknown metaphysical planes and the academic bowl team captain stops to grab his instruction manual? Let me guess, Van AssMan. You died of boredom in your last life, right?"

Zelda turned and looked right at Martin, the jewel hanging from her golden circlet flashing at him. "You are the biggest nerd I never met in my life," she said with a frown.

"Whatever," Martin answered.

He'd already started flipping to a chapter called, "Exiting the Soul Reassignment Office."

"Maybe I'm the nerd who can't leave a book behind or maybe I'm the brains behind this operation, holding a wealth of information at my fingertips. You decide. I'll be over here on this other rock, reading everything we need to know about being ghosts."

Martin strode/glided clumsily off to one side and tried to sit down on a large rock with his back to the others. He couldn't quite sit, of course, so his butt ended up hovering above the rock's flat top. He folded his legs up under him, somewhat aware that he looked like a cartoon genie, but he didn't care. His eyes were already skimming the chapter about leaving the Soul Reassignment Office, and he didn't like what he was reading.

Zelda came up behind Martin and put a hand on his shoulder. That, at least, he could feel, and he liked it.

"So, Brainiac," she said. "What does it say about sneaking out through the portal?"

Martin looked at her, too concerned to hold a grudge. "It basically says we shouldn't, under any circumstances, do it."

"Why not?" Now Zeke was coming over, too.

"Well," Martin said. "For one thing, without a new assignment, we're basically here as ghosts."

Zeke snorted. "Yeah," he said. "We'd already figured that much out."

"But there's more," Martin told him. "Out here? Away from the office? We're what the manual calls the verloren."

"Verloren?" Zeke peered over Martin's shoulder at the dense text.

"It's German," Martin said. "It means lost."

Zelda raised her eyebrows at him.

"What?" Martin said. "I studied German. And French and Spanish. I liked languages, OK?"

"Whatever," she said. She shook her head and looked like she felt sorry for him. "So, we're verloren. So what?"

"Lost souls," Zeke said. "Souls without an assignment. That's heavy." He pretended to skip another stone.

"Right," said Martin. "Lost souls. We don't belong anywhere."

"Well, that sounds pretty sweet to me," Zeke said. "Maybe this is the break in the cycle I've been looking for. I think I'm going to like not belonging anywhere for a while."

Martin cleared his throat. "Except it says here in the book that lost souls are periodically rounded up."

"Rounded up?" Zelda said.

"Yeah. They have a staff of Seekers from the Soul Reassignment Office, it says, who help lost souls—mostly those who experienced some kind of a complication immediately following their deaths—get back to the office and prepare for their new assignments."

"So we don't have much time?" Zelda said. "I still want to see my family."

"I don't know," Martin said. "But there's something else. It says here that the Seekers' primary objective is to guide the verloren back to the office before they're claimed by someone else."

"Who?" Zelda's eyes were wide.

Martin shut the book. "Eh," he said. "You know what? It doesn't matter. Let's just try to get back to the office as fast as possible."

Zelda grabbed the book out of his hands. "Who?" she yelled, flipping frantically through the pages. "Who is coming to claim our lost souls?"

"Satan," Zeke said.

Zelda gasped and clutched her throat, letting Martin's manual fall to the rocks, where it hovered just an inch above them. "Is it true?" she asked Martin.

"You doubt me?" Zeke said angrily.

"Well, he's the one who read the book!" Zelda shouted.

"It's true," Martin said. "He's right. According to the manual, the verloren are easy prey for Satan. Once the demons get a hold of you, the Soul Reassignment Office can't do much to help. The book says they can file an appeal with Hell's front office, but…come on. An appeal? To Hell? That's ludicrous."

"What's ludicrous," said Zeke. "Is someone your age using the word ludicrous!"

"Said the King of Ludicrousticity!" Zelda yelled at him.

"That's not a word." Martin sighed.

"Oh my God!" Zelda moaned. "I can't believe it!"

"Really," Martin assured her. "That's not a real word. Not in any language."

"Not that!" she yelled. "The demons! They could be here at any minute!" She started tearing up then, flinging herself at Martin, who stood up clumsily from his fake-seated position and gathered her up in his insubstantial arms.

"It'll be OK," he said, even though he didn't see how it possibly could be.

"Sure it will," Zelda snapped in between deep breaths. "They're just demons, right. No biggie." Her body trembled against Martin's in spite of her bravado. He rubbed her back in what he hoped was a consoling way.

"Hey!" Zeke yelled. "Fartin Van AssMan! What's it going to take for you to keep your damned verloren hands off my girlfriend?"

Zelda let go of Martin and spun around to face Zeke. "You know we're broken up, right?" she yelled.

"What?" Zeke said, plainly shocked. "Because of this book-toting turd?"

"No!" she yelled. "Because you killed me!"

"Whoa!" Martin said, stumble-floating away from the two of them. "You did?" he asked Zeke. "Did you murder her?"

"He did!" Zelda answered.

"Psssht." Zeke made a dismissive noise with his mouth. "It wasn't murder! I was doing you a favor!"

"Some favor!" Zelda said. "Thanks a whole fucking lot!"

"You hated your life!" Zeke said.

"I did not!" Zelda was defiant.

"Well, you said it, like, five times a day!" Zeke used a falsetto voice to imitate Zelda. "Oh, Zeke, I hate my life! I hate our stupid school! I hate my family! I hate my parents! My sister's such a little bitch! Life sucks so much! I just hate my whole life!"

"That's not how I sounded!" Zelda roared. "And I didn't mean it!"

"Well, how was I supposed to know?"

"Because everybody says shit like that! That's just normal teen angst!"

"Did you say shit like that?" Zeke asked Martin, who really didn't want to be a part of the conversation.

"Well, I. Uh. Well. No, not really," he admitted. Zelda glared at him. "But, you know," he added. "I can see where someone else would. I mean, I'd say that I hated my parents, too, if they'd named me Zelda Kozikowski."

Zeke convulsed with laughter.

Zelda fumed.

"They didn't name her Zelda," Zeke said between guffaws. "They named her Jane. Plain fucking Jane. She had it changed at the courthouse last year."

"What?" Martin was in serious danger of freaking out. He was a lost soul, Satan's minions might be hot on his trail, and his only company at the moment was a potential murderer and someone he knew only by an alias.

"So what?" Zelda said. "So I changed my name. A lot of people do it!"

Martin sighed and ran a hand through his short hair. "Just tell me it was because of Zelda Fitzgerald," he said. "Just tell me that and I'll forget all about it."

Zelda looked down at the rocks below her hovering feet.

"It was because of the video game," Zeke said matter-of-factly. "The Legend of Zelda."

"I told you I was a gamer chick," Zelda said.

"Well," Martin said. "I can't say I'm not disappointed."

"Add it to the list," Zeke said. "The ever-growing list of disappointing things that have happened since you became one of the verloren, doomed to wander the Earth forever—at best."

"You're right," Martin said. "We've got bigger problems right now than teen angst and identity crises."

"No," Zeke said. "You know what? You've got bigger problems. I'm done with problems. I've had fifty-nine lifetimes of problems and I'm all problemed out. You," he pointed at Zelda. "Broke up with me. And you," he pointed at Martin. "Are in over your head with this drama queen, but whatever. Good luck to you. Both of you. I'm out of here."

"Zeke!" Zelda shouted, going after him. "You can't leave!"

"I can, and I am!" Zeke said. He kept walking along the rocks.

"We should probably stick together," Martin called after him. "You know, safety in numbers and all that."

Zeke held his middle finger up over his shoulder and kept walking.

Zelda fell to the rocks dramatically and screamed skyward in anger The effect was somewhat ruined by the fact that she hovered above the ground, which made her look far less fierce than she imagined. She must have realized this and seen that her theatrics were lost on the retreating Zeke, because when he failed to turn around and acknowledge them, she scowled at his back and returned his one-finger salute.

Martin wasn't exactly sorry to see Zeke go. He wasn't sure a guy who'd kill his own girlfriend was the best company to keep in the afterlife. But he wondered whether Zeke was right about him being in over his head with Zelda. First, Zeke had killed this girl and then his lost soul had abandoned hers. If she was too much for a tough guy like Zeke, she was definitely too much for a geek like Martin. And Zelda had made it plain that Martin wasn't her ideal afterlife companion, either. Now, they were apparently stuck with each other whether they liked it or not.

Martin sighed and walked over to where Zelda still floated above the ground, her skirts splayed out around her. Together, they watched Zeke disappear around the bend.

"Come on," Martin said when Zelda seemed to have calmed down a little. "Get up. We'll be OK without him. We can figure this out together."

"Yeah, OK." Zelda sniffed and stood up. She dusted off her skirts even though they'd never technically touched the ground. "He'll be back," she said. "He'll totally be back."

Chapter 4

Zeke didn't come back. Martin and Zelda waited on the rocky shoreline throughout the night, but there was no sign of him. Technically, they didn't need to sleep, but when darkness fell they lay down anyway out of habit. Their bodies hovered an inch above the rocks and shivered with unfelt cold as they closed eyes that would never tire. They didn't talk, though they both obviously had a lot of unspoken thoughts coursing through their minds. It was one of the longest nights of Martin's life. Or, rather, his life and his afterlife combined.

When the sun began to rise, Martin sat up. He saw that Zelda had gone to stand at the water's edge, where the newly awoken sun was making orange ripples on its surface. With the light at that angle, he could see right through her, saw the water shimmering and sparkling through her big medieval gown. She took a few small, tentative steps offshore, floating out over the water. She walked slowly along a beam of new-day sunlight, following it a couple hundred yards out onto the water. Then she stood there, perfectly silhouetted against the big orange orb as it rose in the sky.

Martin stood up, entranced. She was beautiful. Suddenly, right there, right then, her dress made sense. She made sense. She was perfect. Martin felt his own ghostly form tremble. He loved her. Zelda, Jane, whoever she was. He loved this goddess of the sun.

Zelda turned and made her way back to shore, following the ever-widening beam of light that had borne her out onto the water. The closer she got, the less shaky Martin felt. What was left of her make-up was hopelessly smeared around her eyes. The jewel she wore on her forehead struck Martin as fairly ridiculous, and the petulant look on her face wasn't exactly the divinely serene expression Martin had been expecting. He sighed and sat back down above the rocks. Just like that, he was out of love. *Oh well,* he thought. *It was beautiful while it lasted.*

"He didn't come back," Zelda said when she reached the shore.

"I'd noticed," Martin replied. He almost stopped himself from asking his next question, but then he figured he had nothing to lose. "Did you really want him to?"

Zelda shrugged. "Yes and no," she said.

"The no, I get," Martin told her. "The yes? Enlighten me."

Zelda sat down next to Martin. They hovered next to each other in silence for a second while she gathered her skirts around her and, presumably, her thoughts.

"I love him," Zelda said. "Or, I thought I did? I don't know now. I don't know anything anymore."

Having only experienced his first taste of love mere moments ago and having had it evaporate as quickly as it had come, Martin wasn't super-impressed by Zelda's declaration.

"He was kind of a pain in the ass, though, right?" Martin ventured.

Zelda laughed. "Totally. But you only knew him at the Soul Reassignment Office. He was super-pissed, obviously, about having to go back there. On Earth, he could be…sweet."

"Sweet?" Hadn't Zeke called him Fartin Van AssMan right here on Earth just yesterday? He hadn't seemed to sweeten up any when they all stepped through the portal.

"Like, sweet in a brooding way, I guess," Zelda said. "He bought me this." She touched the gold circlet on her head.

"It's nice," Martin lied. He felt like he should say something more about it. "It really classes up the wench outfit," he said.

Zelda shot him a look. "I'm not a wench. I'm a lady in waiting."

"My mistake," Martin said. "Sorry."

"You should be," she told him.

"Well, I am."

Zelda sighed. "Zeke just got me," she said. "Maybe it wasn't healthy. I don't know. We were both pissed off. I was pissed off about trivial little things on Earth, I guess, and his grudge turned out to be against the whole of the universe, but, at our cores, we were both just a couple of pissed-off people who sometimes made each other feel better."

"OK," Martin said.

Zelda looked up and down the shoreline. "He really didn't come back."

"No, he didn't."

They were quiet again.

"Can I ask you something?" Martin said.

"What?"

"You said Zeke killed you. Was it true?"

Zelda didn't answer.

"I'm not trying to pry or anything," Martin said. "It's just…if he does come back…I mean, I'd like to know what we're dealing with."

Zelda sighed again. "He killed me," she said. "But I let him."

"Why?"

"I don't know," Zelda said. She looked like she might cry again. "It's like Zeke was saying, I guess. I was a bit theatrical at times. I'd go on and on about how pissed off I was about everything—stupid stuff, I can see now: my parents favoring my sister or some idiots saying something dumb to me at school—and Zeke would say, 'Babe, you can get off the ride anytime you want.' And I'd be like, 'Don't be such a dick.' So, one day, after we'd been together for about eight months, Zeke tells me how he's lived fifty-nine lives and all of them have been shit. At first, I freaked out, right? I was all like, 'Oh, shit. My boyfriend's fucking nuts.' But he stuck to his story and after a while, I kind of believed him. I dunno why. I guess I just wanted to. I leaned on him, you know? He always seemed to know what to do. I liked the way he acted like nothing mattered. It felt…refreshing, you know? Made me feel free."

Zelda sighed and looked out over the water. The magic of the sunrise was gone. The morning had become completely ordinary.

"So, anyway," Zelda said. "This one day, we were driving to a Renaissance festival. It was kind of a long drive; they can be sort of hard to find. This one was out of state. The whole thing was my idea, of course, because Zeke never made any plans or anything, thinking as he did that anything and everything was futile." Zelda smiled ruefully. "Zeke wouldn't talk about any of his past lives, but he must have lived through the real Renaissance, and being dragged to those kinds of festivals probably slayed him. He went along with it for my sake, though, agreed to drive and everything. He liked me in this costume." Zelda looked down modestly. "He said I looked ravishing."

Martin nodded. Even a jerk like Zeke would have to enjoy the view at the top of that corset.

"So, we were just driving along and Zeke started in on one of his rants about how shitty human life is and I wanted to be supportive so I was all like, 'Oh, yeah, babe. I totally know. Like, I hate it here. I can't wait to get out.' I kind of meant college, you know, like I couldn't wait to get out of town, get away from my parents, and just start over in college. But Zeke heard something different because he was like, 'We can get out right now!' I was thinking he meant running away, which sounded fun and we were kind of doing it anyway because we were already on the road, so I was like, 'Yeah. We should totally get out. We should just leave all those stupid fucks behind.' Zeke was the happiest I'd ever seen him. He was smiling and driving fast. Really fast. 'How about there?' he said. We were coming up on a huge field with a big lake in the middle of it. I was like, 'Yeah, sure, babe. Whatever.' I was thinking it would have been more fun to go on to the festival, but whatever. A lake day could be fun, too, you know? Maybe a little skinny dipping? Making out on the shore? Just plain old fun, you know?"

"I know," Martin said, even though he didn't. He'd never had that kind of fun when he was alive. He wished he could get the image of Zeke skinny dipping out of his mind.

"But, that's not what Zeke meant. He started accelerating, driving off the road and heading toward this huge lake. I was like, 'Babe! What the fuck are you doing?' 'We're getting out,' he said. 'This is what you wanted!' And I realized what he was thinking, and I was like, 'Oh, what? You're just going to end it all right now?' And we were flying across the grass, heading right toward the water, and he was like, 'Are you chickening out?' There wasn't time to say anything except, 'No! But…' before we flew over this huge bank and landed right in the middle of the lake. And I was like, 'Damn it. My dress is going to get wet.' That's it. That's all I thought. I figured the whole thing was just a big inconvenience. And I was actually glad, you know, that I hadn't told Zeke to stop, that I hadn't chickened out on him. Then, we started sinking."

Martin was really starting to hate this story.

"It happened so fast," Zelda said. "One minute, we were floating there, kind of peacefully, the next, there was water rushing in everywhere. I couldn't get my seatbelt off. I was like, 'Zeke! Zeke, help me!' but he was just sitting there, not even trying to escape, laughing his head off as the water poured over his lap. I finally got my buckle undone, but by then the car was almost totally submerged. I couldn't open the door. Zeke wasn't laughing anymore. I couldn't look at him. I tried to kick out the window, the windshield. Nothing." Zelda held out a foot shod in a velveteen medieval-looking slipper for Martin to see. "Stupid shoes," she said. "Useless. And, I suspect, rather inauthentic, too." Zelda sighed and shook her head. "Anyway, I held my breath as long as I could, but then I couldn't anymore. The water had looked so pretty when we'd been driving toward it, but in my mouth it tasted ugly. Muddy, dirty, metallic even. That's what I remember most, that disgusting taste. I'm sure it didn't take me that long to drown, but it felt like forever."

Martin pulled his hood up over his head to ward off a chill he knew came from within and was completely silent. That's the only thing one can be after hearing a story like that.

Zelda fiddled with her slipper. "That was a long answer to a short question," she said. "Basically, yeah, Zeke killed me, but I kind of gave him permission."

"That doesn't make it OK," Martin said.

"Maybe not." Zelda shrugged. "He knew about the Soul Reassignment Office, though. It's not like he killed me and had no idea what would happen to me. He knew I'd be fine, go on to another life."

"He also must have known that you had a purpose to fulfill on Earth, and he didn't give you a chance to do that."

"True."

"So, you're not mad at him? Seriously?"

"I guess I am." Zelda thought a minute. "I definitely am. But I feel sorry for him, too."

They looked up and down the shoreline some more.

"He really didn't come back," Zelda said again.

"No," Martin said. "He didn't. And, I don't want to freak you out or anything, but if there really are demons out looking for us, we might want to get moving."

"Agreed," Zelda said. "Does the manual say anything about traveling the Earth as a couple of verloren?"

Martin picked up the book and scanned the index. He turned some pages, skimmed some of the text. "Not really," he said. "It just says we can't interact with the physical world here, which we'd pretty much already figured out. It mentions the demons a few times, of course." They both looked around nervously before Martin turned back to the book. "And," he said. "It expressly cautions the verloren from returning to the places where they lived out their Earthly lives."

"But that's exactly what we came here to do," Zelda said.

"Yeah," said Martin. "I know. But the book says that nothing good can come of it. Time will have passed. The people we left behind won't be the same. Look. It says right here that verloren who become obsessed with the affairs of the living bind themselves to their Earthly dwelling places, denying their souls the opportunity to be reassigned. The result is what humans call a haunting, and it's detrimental to the souls of both the verloren and the humans involved."

"But we're totally still doing it anyway, right?" Zelda asked.

"I guess so." Martin sighed. "But can we please make a deal? I won't let you become obsessed with the affairs of the living and you do the same for me?"

"Deal," Zelda said. She looked at the rocky shoreline again. "Now where on Earth do you suppose we are?"

Chapter 5

Martin had hoped they hadn't traveled too far from the places they'd died, and he'd been right. The back of his manual listed tons of regional Soul Reassignment Offices. He and Zelda, as luck would have it, had only lived a couple towns apart when they were alive and so, Martin theorized, had both wound up in the same regional office when they died. The shoreline on which they'd landed, it turned out, was part of a state park along a bay only about a hundred miles from Martin's parents' house. They found this out not in any otherworldly way, of course. They just walked inland until they came to the Bay State Park entrance and looked at the maps and signage that were conveniently placed there. Taking in some of the park's hiking trails and recreation areas, Martin thought he vaguely remembered a childhood day full of picnicking and swimming on one of the sand beaches at the other end of the park. The happy memory made him extraordinarily sad. He knew it was clichéd, but he really had forgotten to appreciate the little things in life.

A hundred miles would have been a lot to cover on foot for human Martin and Zelda, but their verloren incarnations did not fatigue. They moved swiftly without even the friction of their footsteps to slow them down, and they easily traversed the distance, arriving on the outskirts of Martin's town just as the sun set. They'd decided to visit Martin's former home first because it was closer. Martin felt a growing sense of unease as they entered his hometown.

The familiarity of the streets felt wrong to him. He belonged there and he didn't. He almost wished they hadn't come.

They were quiet as they approached Martin's development, Zelda hanging back a bit to let Martin lead the way. They stuck to the sidewalks even though they could have run down the middle of the street without worrying about the dangers posed by traffic. Martin wanted to turn back, but he felt himself being drawn toward his old house. The desire to see what had transpired in his absence was too great to be ignored.

Soon, they were turning down the cul-de-sac where Martin had learned to ride a bike. There was Harper Hanson's house, with the pool in the back where Martin was sometimes invited to swim as a child. There was old Mr. Schadmire's house; he used to turn the hose on kids who trespassed on his property. Sometimes, on the hottest summer days, they'd bait him on purpose, then laugh and laugh as he cooled them off with big jets of icy water. Inevitably, Martin found himself pacing back and forth at the edge of his driveway.

"This is it," he said to Zelda. He waved his arms a little spastically in the direction of his childhood home.

"Nice," she said, even though the house was a perfectly ordinary three-bedroom just like every other house on the street.

"Thanks," Martin said, stopping to really look at the house. He supposed it was nice, all things considered. He had just never properly appreciated it.

"Are we going in?" Zelda asked.

"I don't know," Martin said. He forced his hands into the pocket of his sweatshirt to keep them still. "I really want to, and I really don't, too. I mean, what if my parents are prostrate with grief? What if my mother is wasting away to nothing and my father's broken beyond all recognition? I was their only child. I was all they had. I don't know if I can handle seeing them like this."

"Then what are we doing here?"

Martin shrugged. "I guess as much as I don't want to see them, I do want to, too."

Zelda nodded. "Want me to go ahead of you?" she offered. "Scout it out? I could let you know what you're in for, at least. Try to soften the blow."

Martin sighed. "That's sweet," he said. "Really. But, I think I just have to go in and see for myself."

"OK," Zelda said. "Do you want me to come? Or should I wait here?"

"Come," Martin said quietly. "Please come."

They glided toward the house. Martin wasn't exactly sure how this was going to work. They approached the door uncertainly. Martin raised one fist.

"You're not going to try to knock, are you?" asked Zelda.

Martin flushed. "No," he said. But, yeah, of course he'd been thinking about knocking.

"We're ghosts, remember?" Zelda said. She glided full-speed toward the white-painted wood siding and disappeared through the wall.

Martin took a deep breath and followed. Passing through the wall was unpleasantly like, well, passing through a solid wall. Luckily, it was over quickly and the discomfort of it was soon forgotten in the swell of emotion that came as Martin once again found himself in his childhood home.

The foyer was dark. He gestured for Zelda to follow him and they drifted down the hall.

"Hello?" Martin called, his voice shaky. "Mom? Dad?"

"They can't hear you, remember?" Zelda said.

"I know," Martin said. And he did. He'd just been hoping, that's all. "How long do you think it's been?" he asked Zelda. "They wouldn't have moved, would they?"

Zelda shrugged.

In the kitchen, evidence of recent meal preparation littered the usually tidy stovetop and counter. The wall calendar showed a date two months past Martin's death. "Eight weeks," Martin whispered to Zelda. "I've been gone eight weeks! It feels like two days!"

"Zeke always said time was meaningless on the other side," she said with a shrug, not bothering to lower her voice.

"I hear something!" Martin said. Voices and the clinking of dishes were muffled in the background. "This way!"

He led Zelda down another short hallway. Behind a glass door covered in sheer white curtains, a soft light glowed. The voices were louder now. Somebody laughed. If Martin weren't already dead, he'd have sworn that he was about to have a heart attack. The anticipation of seeing what was on the other side of the door was, figuratively speaking, killing him. He summoned all of his courage and forced his ghostly form through the door. He found himself standing in his parents' dining room. In a moment, Zelda was right beside him.

All of Martin's wild imaginings about what it might be like to see his parents again did nothing to prepare him for that moment. There was his mother, as elegant as ever, in an ivory blouse and a pearl necklace, sipping a glass of white wine. His father, in a handsome suit and tie, was laughing at a joke Martin must have just missed. He went and stood right behind them, trying to put a ghostly arm around each of them and failing. Zelda looked at him with sympathy.

Also at the table were the Mortimers, Irene and Paul, business associates of Martin's father who had come to dinner a few times a year when Martin was alive. How he had hated those dinners, sitting there in his buttoned-up collar, watching his parents suck up to the snooty Mortimers and their horrible son who was several years older and at least as many inches taller than Martin. Not to mention the fact that he was the captain of every kind of sports team in the Western hemisphere. The Boy Wonder was absent from the dinner table now, of course, being off at some prestigious university somewhere—the kind of institution to which Martin had always dreamed of applying—on a sports scholarship.

"That's hysterical, Paul," Martin's father was saying. "What did you do next?"

"Well," Paul said, setting Martin's grandmother's finest silverware on the edge of his plate and leaning forward. "I let him have it!"

Now both of Martin's parents were laughing.

"You didn't!" Martin's mother said. "You just…gave it to him?"

"What could I do?" Paul said with a chuckle.

Irene rolled her eyes and took a long sip of her drink. "I can think of lots of things you could have done, Paul," she said. "Besides giving the sheikh your brand-new Rolex!"

Paul waved off his wife's comment. "He really seemed to like it. I can't help it if we had some miscommunication. My Arabic was rusty; I had no idea what he was really asking me until it was too late. The main thing is, I got that contract signed. I can buy a million Rolexes just from my cut of that one deal alone. And I'm sure there are going to be plenty more contracts where that one came from."

"That's hardly the point," Irene said. "Think of the great disservice you did the man—the great disservice you did your whole country. He said something along the lines of, 'Can I have the time?' and you handed him a $10,000 watch. He's going to think Americans are all dreadfully stupid or entirely too rich and careless, both awful stereotypes I should think you wouldn't want to perpetuate."

"That's true," Martin's mother said, nodding. "But still, I think it's a lovely example of diplomacy in action. Imagine if world leaders treated each other with such goodwill and generosity every time there was some sort of misunderstanding. All the world's problems would be solved. Now, who wants some dessert?" She stood up and started clearing dishes from the table. Martin followed her as she opened the dining-room door and headed to the kitchen. She deposited the plates on the counter and leaned against it for a minute, breathing deeply. Martin had always suspected his mother didn't like the Mortimers much. Now he had proof!

"Mom?" he said. "Mom?"

Martin's mother straightened up at the counter.

Had she heard him?

"Mom! Mom! It's me! It's Martin!"

Martin's mother took a deep breath, then turned to face him.

Then, she reached right through him to open the refrigerator and take out a big pink bakery box. Martin watched her stack gorgeous éclairs on a fine china platter, take another deep breath, paste her best hostess-with-the-mostess smile on her face, and head back down the hallway. "Dessert is served!" he heard her call cheerily.

"Martin?" Zelda said. "Don't you want to follow her?"

"What's the point?" Martin said. "So we can watch them stuff their faces with my favorite dessert and laugh about some idiot's shitty Arabic?"

"I don't get it," Zelda said. "You should be happy. Nobody's prostrate with grief after all."

"Exactly!" said Martin. "I was their only child! How could they not be prostrate with grief?"

"Wait," Zelda said. "You mean, you wanted them to be miserable?"

"Yes!" Martin wailed. "Or, no. I don't know! But I didn't want them to be eating éclairs!"

"Oh, so what? Martin's dead so nobody on Earth can eat éclairs anymore?"

"No!" Martin said. "OK, yes! Alright? Yes! They should be too sad to eat éclairs ever again."

Zelda hurried out into the hallway and stuck her head through the dining-room wall. She looked ridiculous there, with her red-skirted bottom sticking out of the hallway wall like that. It was almost enough to make Martin smile.

Zelda pulled her head out of the wall and came back to stand next to Martin. "If it makes you feel any better," she said. "Your mother has only taken one bite of hers."

"And the others?" Martin asked hopefully.

"They seem to be enjoying them," Zelda reported. "Especially that guy Paul. He's on his second one."

"Dick," Martin said.

Zelda smiled.

"Should we get out of here?" Martin asked. "Before I become too obsessed with the éclairs or whatever and bind myself to this dwelling place for all eternity?"

"I dunno," Zelda said. "Maybe you should wait until the party's over?"

"I don't think so." Martin sighed.

"Well," Zelda said. "Don't you want to see your old room or anything?" She made exaggerated flirty eyes at him. "You could at least take me up to see your room."

Martin gave Zelda a little shove. "Cut it out," he said. "No, I don't see any point in visiting my old room. They've probably already made it over."

"Yeah," Zelda said. "They've probably turned it into a walk-in refrigerator for the piles of éclairs they eat every single night."

Martin snickered in spite of himself. "Let's just get out of here," he said with a smile.

"OK," Zelda said. She took his hand and he let her and, out of habit, he led her toward the front door.

Just as Martin was about to force himself to walk
through the heavy steel door, Zelda gasped and jerked him
backwards.

"What?" he said, irritated. His brain didn't seem to be
doing its job at the moment. Used to memorizing trivia and
finding derivatives, it just wasn't flexible enough to wrap
itself around the fact that his parents were entertaining the
Mortimers, serving them éclairs and allowing themselves to
be amused by Paul's stupid anecdotes in spite of the fact
that their one and only son was dead.

Martin just wanted to leave.

"Look," Zelda said, pulling him toward the hallway
table. There, right in the middle of the foyer, was a framed
eight-by-ten photo of Martin. It was his school picture; he'd
worn a shirt and tie for the occasion. Around the photo were
tiny easels displaying a mass card and a laminated copy of
his obituary. Fresh flowers filled a vase that stood behind
the photo.

"Wow," Martin said.

"It's a shrine," Zelda said. "A shrine to Martin Van
Assen."

"Huh," Martin said. He skimmed his brief obituary. It
said he'd been the Recording Secretary of the Language
Arts Society. He sighed. He'd actually been promoted to
Treasurer that year and now the world would never know.

"So, does this make you feel better?" Zelda asked.

"I guess so," Martin said.

"Can people enjoy their éclairs guilt-free now that
Martin Van Assen has been properly memorialized in their
foyer?"

"Yeah. Sure," said Martin. "I mean, I guess I just wanted to know that they remembered me."

Martin heard his mother's party-perfect voice in the hallway again. "Excuse me just a minute," she was saying. "I'll be right back."

They heard her shoes click along the hardwood floors and onto the tile of the hallway bathroom. A door shut quickly, a faucet was turned on, and then the unmistakable sound of retching drifted into the foyer.

"She couldn't stomach the éclairs!" Martin said, unable to suppress a grin.

"You asshole," Zelda said. "You're actually happy about this? You want her to be sick with grief? You'd deny her even the simple pleasure of a chocolate-covered, cream-filled dessert? Well, maybe she's not sad at all! Maybe she's pregnant, huh? Maybe that's why she's puking. Maybe she's pregnant with your replacement already. Have you ever considered that?"

"No," Martin said, looking crestfallen.

More retching came from the bathroom.

"Can we please go now?" Martin said. He didn't wait for Zelda's permission. He just took off through the wall and assumed that she would follow. Neither of them spoke as they glided back up Martin's street in the dark.

Zelda finally broke the silence. "I'm sorry for what I said."

"It's OK," Martin sighed. "You were probably right."

"I wasn't," Zelda said. "I was just being mean."

"Whatever."

"Seriously, Martin, she's not pregnant, alright? You were right, you little egomaniac. She couldn't stomach the dessert."

"You can't know that for sure," Martin said.

"The wine," Zelda said. "She was drinking wine with her dinner. Pregnant women don't do that."

"Oh," Martin said. He tried not to seem relieved or happy in any way.

"Really," Zelda said. "I'm sorry. They miss you, Martin. I could tell. Nobody keeps a shrine to someone they don't miss."

"Thanks," Martin said.

"People grieve in different ways, you know? Some people drink or gamble, some visit grave sites, some yell and scream. Some people waste away to nothing, some people eat éclairs."

"OK," Martin said. "I get it. Can we please stop talking about this?"

"I'll try," Zelda said. "But I'm really, really in the mood for an éclair right now."

Chapter 6

It was night by the time they reached Zelda's neighborhood. Martin tried to talk her out of going, of course. "The book was right," he said. "Seeing my parents' lives without me was detrimental to my soul!"

But Zelda didn't listen.

"It's not the same for me," she said. "I'm totally fine with them all going on without me. In fact, that's what I need to see."

"What if that's just what you *think* you need to see?" Martin said. "What if when you really see it, it freaks you the fuck out and makes you feel like your whole life was totally meaningless?"

"Your life wasn't meaningless," Zelda said.

"I know that!" Martin shouted, waving his arms just a little frantically. "Don't you think I know that?"

They glided through the darkness in silence then, Martin watching the ground fly by beneath his feet, brooding. He was still thinking about the éclairs, the shrine, and what, if anything, it all might or might not have meant.

Suddenly, Zelda stopped and grabbed his arm. "That's it," she said. "There it is."

Martin looked at the house. There were lots of lights on inside combatting the darkness and a TV flickered in a downstairs window. The two-story house with plain blue vinyl siding and brick front steps looked far too ordinary to have housed the lady-in-waiting Zelda who wore a jeweled circlet and bright-red Renaissance dress. There was a neat little flower bed on each side of the porch and an asphalt driveway that looked like it had recently been resealed. The mailbox at the end of the driveway had a daisy painted on it.

Zelda saw Martin eyeing the daisy on the mailbox. "I did that," she said, her voice barely above a whisper. "My sister helped. We painted it as a Mother's Day present for my mom, years ago."

Zelda reached out to run her fingers over the well-worn paint, but couldn't actually touch it. She looked up at the house again, her resolve to go inside apparently weakening.

Martin squared his shoulders and sighed. "Are you sure you want to do this?" he asked Zelda.

"Yes," she said.

Martin started forward.

"Only…" Zelda held him back. "Not at night."

"What?"

"It's creepy," Zelda said. "Slinking around in the night like a ghost. Can't we wait until morning?"

"May I remind you that you *are* a ghost?" Martin asked her.

"You may not!"

"Are you kidding me with this right now?"

"No," Zelda said. "Please? Please can't we wait until it's daylight? Please? I want to see them moving on with their lives, not vegging out to prime-time TV in their pajamas and stuffing their faces with junk."

Martin sighed. He thought about how he wished he hadn't seen his family eating éclairs.

"Seriously, Martin, what else do you have to do right now? What's a few more hours?"

"Fine," Martin said. "Fine." He looked over his shoulder. None of Hell's demons seemed to be pursuing them through the quiet streets of Zelda's suburban neighborhood. "I guess we can hang out for a little while."

"Thank you," Zelda said.

They stared at the house together.

"Are you sure we can't go in?" Martin finally asked. "I could go for a little prime-time TV."

"Shut up," Zelda said. "There's an old swing set out back. Come on."

Zelda led Martin into her backyard, where they hovered side-by-side about an inch above the seat of a two-person glider.

"Well, this is fun," Martin said.

"Shut up," Zelda said again with a small smile.

Martin pretended to swing. His ghost moved back and forth through the back of the glider, but the swing didn't move. "Whee!" he joked.

Zelda laughed a little. A breeze neither of them could feel rustled the trees and set the glider in motion. It swung back and forth through their middles. Martin sighed. The lack of interaction with the physical world was getting downright depressing.

"You never told me," Zelda said. "How exactly did you die?"

"What?" Martin said.

"Your untimely demise," Zelda said. "How did it happen?"

"Oh," Martin said dismissively. "It wasn't anything special."

"Car accident?" Zelda guessed.

"No," Martin said.

"Hmmm," Zelda said. "OK. Let me see if I can guess. Aneurysm?"

"No."

"A mugging gone bad?"

"In my sleepy little cul-de-sac?"

"Right, OK. Not exactly thug city. Choking, then? Did you choke to death? That's it, isn't it? You choked to death on an éclair!"

"Interesting," Martin said. "But no."

"Ski accident?"

"No."

"Skydiving parachute fail? Deep-water scuba mishap?"

Martin laughed.

"Wait, I know!" Zelda yelled. "You were murdered! By that Woo kid from the academic bowl team! He wanted your place in the championships, so *BAM!* He smashed your skull in with last year's trophy and left you to bleed out in the back of the auditorium!"

"Uhm. No."

"OK," Zelda said. "I give up. You're going to have to tell me."

Martin sighed. "OK," he said. "Well. There was this international film noir festival over at the Cineplex 2000? A couple friends and I had waited hours in line for tickets and we were totally stoked."

Martin paused.

"Go on," Zelda encouraged him.

"I can't," Martin said. "I don't want to. It's too embarrassing. Really."

"Wait," Zelda said. "There's an element of this story that's more embarrassing than the fact that you camped out in line for international film festival tickets? This, I've got to hear."

"We didn't camp out."

"Whatever," she said. "You went. You paid real money for the tickets. That's bad enough. Then what happened?"

"So, we were at the film festival," Martin said with one of his trademark sighs. "And we'd just gotten inside. The first screening was supposed to be Noguerra's *La Luna de Mañana*. Do you know it?"

"Of course not."

"Well, it's this great film, really, about this guy, this private eye with one arm who discovers a serial killer right in his inner circle. But the thing is, the killer has this special kind of amnesia? So, like, he doesn't even remember all the heinous crimes he's committed? And this makes it really hard to pin anything on him because—"

"Could you get to the part where you die, please? Or are you implying that you died of boredom during the screening?"

"Right," Martin said. "OK. So, anyway, I was super excited about the movie, and I didn't want to miss any part of it, so I told my friends to go save me a seat and I went into the restroom before it started."

"And that's where the Woo kid assaulted you to steal your nerd team seat?"

"No." Martin sighed. "That's where I slipped in a puddle of someone else's urine and hit my head on a urinal."

"Wow," Zelda said. "I can see why you don't go around bragging about that."

"Yeah," Martin said. "Thanks."

They hovered just above the swing in silence for a few minutes.

"Hey," Zelda said. "It must be some comfort that you ended up in the waiting room of the Soul Reassignment Office, right?"

"How do you figure?" Martin asked.

"I mean, like, obviously you weren't meant to go that way. Or you would have been one of the stiffs with an appointment. You wouldn't have had to wait."

"Huh," Martin said. "I hadn't thought about it like that. I guess, yeah, it is somewhat nice to think that my whole life wasn't destined to lead up to cracking my skull against a public pee receptacle."

"Yeah," Zelda said. "It was just one of those things."

"A freak accident."

"Could have happened to anyone."

"Probably happens all the time."

"Sure," Zelda said. "The Urinal Safety Commission reports that, every year, numbers of people reaching into the low single digits are injured—some fatally—attempting to relieve themselves in public men's rooms."

"Shut up," Martin said.

"The statistics are even higher for dorks at international film festivals."

"OK," Martin said. "You've had your fun."

He and Zelda hovered above the glider without talking or looking at each other. Martin's shoulders started to shake a little, and Zelda reached out to him. "Hey," she said. "I'm sorry. I was only kidding." Then, Martin turned toward her and she breathed a sigh of relief. The nerd who'd slipped in a puddle of pee wasn't crying about it; he was laughing.

Chapter 7

Zelda's family was a bunch of early risers, and Martin was glad because he was bored out of his skull just sitting in their backyard waiting for the sun to come up. A light suddenly illuminated a downstairs window and Zelda, who must have been watching the house for the first signs of morning activity, jumped up and yelled, "The kitchen! They're up!"

Martin stretched even though he wasn't really cramped, and stood up. "Let's roll," he said.

"Um."

"Oh," Martin said, sitting back down on the glider swing. "I can wait here if you want. That's cool."

"No," Zelda said. "It's not that. I'm just…"

"Nervous?"

"Scared shitless."

"You don't have to do this," Martin said. "In fact, it's probably much better if you don't."

"No," Zelda said, squaring her shoulders. "I'm going in." She started gliding toward the house. A couple more windows had been illuminated now and one of them cast an eerie patch of light across the grass, which Zelda glided through unseen. She stopped and looked back at Martin. "Aren't you coming?" she asked.

"What? Oh, yeah." Martin said. "I mean, I can. If you want me to."

"Please," Zelda said, and Martin drifted up alongside her. She took his ghostly hand in hers and together they pressed themselves through the wall of the kitchen.

Martin blinked in the sudden brightness. Not only were all the kitchen lights on, but the entire room was yellow. Martin felt like he had just landed on the sun. He couldn't believe the perpetually pissed-off Zelda had regularly taken her meals somewhere so cheerful and pleasant.

"Look, they're up!" Zelda hissed.

"You don't have to whisper," Martin said in his normal voice. "They can't hear you, remember? Oh, look! Omelets!"

"My mother was always big on breakfast," Zelda whispered.

"Seriously, Zelda, cut it out with the whispering. It's giving me the creeps. Watch." Martin passed his not-quite-opaque hand back and forth in front of Mrs. Kozikowski's face. "Hello!" he shouted. "Hello! See?" He turned to Zelda. "Nothing."

"Stop it right now, Van AssMan. Don't harass them!"

"I'm not harassing anybody!" Martin said. "That's my whole point!" But he moved away from Zelda's mom. At least his verloren friend wasn't whispering anymore.

A man in corduroy pants and a bulky sweater came into the kitchen. "Morning," he greeted his wife.

"Daddy!" Zelda said, then blushed.

Martin looked away, embarrassed on her behalf. He scanned the side of the refrigerator which was papered with family photos, shopping lists, and… and something else. Something bad. Martin resolved not to let Zelda see it under any circumstances.

"Omelet?" Zelda's mom asked her husband.

"Yes, please," he said.

"See?" Martin said to Zelda, grabbing her by the shoulders and turning her back toward the kitchen wall through which they'd entered. "They're doing great. So polite. Eating a hearty breakfast. They're getting along just fine without you. Shall we go?"

"What? No! We just got here."

"Come on," Martin said, pushing Zelda toward the wall. "You've seen what you need to see!"

"Unhand me, Van AssMan!" Zelda broke free of Martin's grip with a theatrical flourish.

"Sorry," Martin mumbled.

"Stop being such a dick or leave," Zelda said. "I wasn't a total asshole when we visited your parents."

"Actually," Martin said. "You kind of were, especially at the end there."

"Shhh," Zelda said, moving back toward the center of the kitchen.

Her mom was cooking at the stove and her father was pouring coffee into an insulated travel mug.

"On second thought," Mr. Kozikowski said. "I'll take a rain check on the eggs. I really need to get going."

"Are you sure you want to put yourself through this again?" Zelda's mother asked him.

"I don't know what else to do," her father said with a shrug. "I know they won't let me help or anything, but at least I can be there to support the volunteers, let them know how grateful we are. They let me hand out water bottles, that kind of thing. At least I'll be there if they find anything."

"OK," Zelda's mother said. "Please let me know if there's anything new."

"Of course," Mr. Kozikowski said. He kissed his wife on the cheek and left the kitchen. Zelda's mom turned off the stove and sighed.

"He must have started some kind of volunteer work?" Zelda said uncertainly. "That's a good thing, right? He's a teacher. Maybe his class is doing a service project? Helping others is a good way to deal with grief, right?"

"Yeah," Martin said. "Totally. He's doing awesome."

"My mom looks tired," Zelda said.

Mrs. Kozikowski was leaning against the counter, her head resting against an upper cabinet.

"Eh," Martin said. "All mothers look like that in the morning."

Zelda's mom stood up a little straighter and smoothed her hair. "Jenny!" she called. "Breakfast is almost ready!"

"Jenny!" Zelda said, and took off. She rushed right past the fridge without stopping to peruse the many papers hanging there, and floated straight up a front staircase.

Martin was right on her heels.

"Who's Jenny?" he asked.

"My sister, duh."

"Oh," Martin said. "Duh." He followed Zelda through a closed bedroom door where an unmade bed and a week's worth of laundry on the floor indicated a teenage occupant.

"Where is she?" Zelda asked, perplexed. She looked around the room again, then ducked back out through the door and into the hallway. She glided along, listening, then stopped in front of an open door. She gasped and her hands fluttered to her face. Martin pulled up short beside her.

"That bitch!" Zelda said. "My room!" Zelda charged through the open door and attempted to confront a girl in nothing but a black lace bra and panties rummaging through the closet. "Hey!" Zelda yelled. "Get out of here! What the hell do you think you're doing?"

The girl didn't hear Zelda, or feel her ghost attempting to physically remove her from the closet doorway. She just stood up on her tiptoes, leg and back muscles taught, looking through a pile of folded t-shirts on the top shelf.

"Can you believe this?" Zelda shouted to Martin.

"No, I can't," he said slowly.

"Hey!" Zelda said, forgetting all about the girl and rushing at Martin. "Stop it!"

"What?" Martin asked.

"Stop looking at her like that!"

"Like what?"

"She's fourteen, you lech!"

"OK," Martin said.

"She's my sister!"

"I get it," Martin said. "Alright. I'm sorry."

Zelda fumed at him another moment, then turned her attention back to the girl in the closet. "Are you kidding me?" she screamed. "Are you fucking kidding me?" She looked at Martin again, her mouth hanging open. "That's my Kid Death t-shirt! She's taking my fucking Kid Death t-shirt! I got that at their last-ever concert! It's signed by the bassist! Look! Right there on the shoulder! It clearly says, 'Tommy Knightshade' in silver Sharpie! It's totally irreplaceable!" When Martin failed to do anything about this grave injustice, Zelda turned back toward her sister. "Give it back! Give it back to me, you little bitch!" She flailed her useless arms at Jenny's face to no avail. Much to Martin's chagrin, Jenny pulled the slightly-too-big-for-her t-shirt over her head, covering up her fancy underwear. "I hate you!" Zelda shrieked at her. "I hate you so fucking much!"

"No, you don't," Martin reminded her sharply. "Remember?"

"Right," Zelda said, breathing hard. "Right."

"Everyone's just moving on here," Martin said calmly. "That's all. OK?"

"OK," Zelda said, sounding calmer. "Moving on. Good. That's good. Moving on is—"

Jenny reached back into the closet and pulled out a pair of leggings with skulls and crossbones printed on them and started to wriggle into them.

"Those are brand-new!" Zelda wailed. "I never even got to wear them!"

"It doesn't matter," Martin reminded her.

"Yes, it does!" Zelda said. "My sister's a looter! She's looting my entire wardrobe!"

"So what?" Martin asked her. "You're done with it."

"Yeah," Zelda said. "I get to wear this stupid thing for all eternity!" She swatted angrily at her medieval costume and looked dangerously close to crying.

"Jenny?" Zelda's mom called from the hallway. She stuck her head into Zelda's room. "What are you doing in here?" She looked her daughter's outfit over with a frown, a manila folder clutched to her chest.

"Just borrowing some clothes," Jenny said. "She always let me wear whatever I wanted of hers."

"Liar!" Zelda growled.

"I don't know," Mrs. Kozikowski said. "I kind of thought we should just leave everything the way she had it."

"Yes!" Zelda screamed.

Jenny looked down at the floor. "I know," she said. "It's just….It makes me feel closer to her to wear her things. You know?"

"Oh, honey!" her mom said, tossing her folder onto the bed so its contents spilled across the bedspread and wrapping Jenny up in a hug. "I do," she cried. "I do know." She was sniffling now, but Jenny was grinning like the Cheshire Cat over her shoulder. "OK," Mrs. Kozikowski said. "Alright. Wear whatever you like. I'm sure your sister would want it that way."

"No! No, I wouldn't!" Zelda shrieked.

Jenny made her face look sad again before pulling away from her mother's embrace. "Thanks, Mom," she said.

Zelda looked like she was going to explode.

Mrs. Kozikowski wiped away a few tears, tried a tentative smile, then said, "Finish getting ready and come down, OK, Jenny? I don't want to be late today." She hastily gathered up her spilled papers. "I have to take these all over town."

"OK," Jenny said. "I'll be right there."

Mrs. Kozikowski hurried back downstairs. Jenny took one last look around the room, stopped in front of Zelda's dresser and scooped up a pair of earrings that were lying there, and hurried out the door as she put them on.

Zelda lunged after her, but Martin held her back. "They're just earrings!" he said. "They don't mean anything."

"They mean something to me," Zelda said, her voice cracking. "It all means something to me." She tried to flop down onto the edge of her bed, but her stubborn defiance of gravity made it impossible. She hovered over her bedspread. Martin joined her. He reached for her hand, then changed his mind and placed his own hands awkwardly in his lap.

"Look," Martin said. "I know how hard it is to see everyone going about their lives without you. But, this is what you wanted. You wanted to see that they're all OK, and they are. Your dad's out and about, your mom's cooking for the family, your sister's being a typical fourteen-year-old girl. You should be happy."

"I should be." Zelda nodded. "You're right. A better person would be thrilled right now. But I'm not a better person. I'm me, and I want everything to go back to the way it was before. Is that so awful?"

"It's not awful," Martin said. "But it's impossible."

"I know that," Zelda said. She started to cry. "It's just…I always said I hated my life, but you know what? I hate my death even more!"

Martin didn't know what to do. He just sat there and let Zelda cry. He looked around the room. The walls were light pink, a shade no doubt left over from Zelda's younger years. Most of the pink was hidden, though, behind dark and ugly band and video-game posters. A few school books were stacked sloppily on the desk and a framed photo of Zelda and Zeke at some kind of costume party stared at Martin. He shifted uncomfortably under its gaze. They were dressed as the video-game characters Link and Zelda, of course, and someone—Zeke, he assumed—had inscribed the wooden frame in black Sharpie. "I only wear elf ears for you, babe!" was followed by a sloppily drawn heart.

"Come on," Martin said gently to Zelda, turning away from the memory-filled room. "We should go."

"I want to stay," Zelda said. "This is where I belong."

"It isn't," Martin said. "Not anymore." He tried to pull Zelda away from the bed, but she resisted. She stretched out across the bedspread, hovering there unnaturally. She rolled over onto her stomach, as if to take a nap, and found her face floating just inches above one of the papers that had fallen out of her mother's file folder. Mrs. Kozikowski must have left it behind in her hurry.

"What the hell is this?" Zelda said, sitting up. She tried to grab the paper, but couldn't. "Martin, look!" she said, on the brink of panic. She scrabbled uselessly at the page. "What the hell is this?"

Martin recognized the paper. He'd seen one like it on the fridge downstairs.

"It's nothing," he said, trying once again to drag Zelda away from her bed and get her out of the house. "Let's go."

"No!" Zelda said. "Look! Martin! Oh my God!"

Martin sighed. "Yeah," he said. "I see."

They both peered at the piece of paper. It was a "Missing" flyer with Zelda's picture in the middle of it.

"Look what my parents put on here!" Zelda shrieked. "Can you believe this? How could they do this to me? I hate them! I fucking hate them!"

Martin furrowed his brow and looked more closely at the flyer. The picture was a school photo. Zelda's skin was shiny, her hair looked kind of flyaway.

"So what?" Martin said, flapping his arms in frustration. "All school photos are awful. And you don't hate your parents, remember?"

"No," Zelda said. "I do! I really do! I wasn't even talking about the photo, you asshole, but thank you very much for saying it's awful."

Martin flinched.

"Look at the name," she said, her voice full of venom. "They put *Jane*. Missing: Jane Kozikowski."

"So what?" Martin said. He'd about had it with Zelda's tumultuous homecoming. He'd have given just about anything to be back in the good old waiting room at the Soul Reassignment Office, sipping a nice hot cup of non-coffee.

"So?" Zelda cried. "So it's not my name! It's disrespectful is what it is! Is that any way to treat a dead girl? Change her name back to her birth name as soon as she's not able to stand up and defend herself anymore?"

"Zelda," Martin said.

"No!" she said. "I mean, seriously. This is the last straw. It's one thing to pilfer a dead girl's clothes and jewelry, but it's quite another to refuse to acknowledge the name that she chose for herself—"

"Zelda."

"A name that she paid her own good money to have legally changed—"

"Zelda."

"I mean, what did those jerks put on my tombstone anyway? I'd like to see. Here lies *Jane*? Rest in peace, *Jane*? It's a fucking insult!"

"Zelda!"

"What?"

"I think you're missing the larger implications of the flyer."

"Oh?" Zelda said.

"It says, 'Missing,'" Martin said. "It's a missing-person flyer."

"Oh," Zelda said. Then, "*Oh!*"

"Yeah."

"Oh my God! Martin! They don't know! They have no idea! They don't know that I'm…"

"Dead."

"Yes!" Zelda sort of staggered through the air, looking around the room a little frantically. "What do they think happened?"

"I don't know," Martin said.

"I bet they think I ran away! Oh my God, Martin! They probably think I left them all on purpose!"

"Well," Martin said quietly. "You kind of did."

"No, I didn't! Not really. Oh!" Zelda flung herself back at the bed. She lay above it for a minute, then sat bolt upright. "We have to tell them," she said.

"Tell them what?"

"That I didn't mean to leave," she said. "That I died. That it was an accident. That…I don't know. That I regret it."

"Sure," Martin said. "Let's just go explain everything to your mom. Or, better yet, we'll just leave them a nice note." He snapped his fingers. "Oh," he said as if he were having a huge revelation. "Except we can't because nobody on Earth can hear or see us and we can't interact with the physical world here at all." Martin headed for Zelda's bedroom wall.

"Come on," he said. "We may as well get the hell out of here."

"No!" Zelda said. "I can't leave them like this. Don't you see? They're not moving on with their lives in the wake of my death. They don't know I'm dead. They're stuck in, like, a limbo of not knowing."

"I know the feeling," Martin muttered.

"I bet that's where my dad was going," Zelda said, close to tears again. "He said something about being there if they found anything. Oh, God, Martin. He hasn't moved on at all. He's out there looking for me right now!"

Martin knew that if he still had a functioning heart it would have been breaking for Zelda and her family. "I'm really sorry," he said.

Zelda shook her head, willing her tears away. "OK," she said. "We have to help them."

"How?" Martin asked.

"The desk," Zelda said. "Look. There's an open notebook right there. And a pencil. In that pencil cup right there. All we have to do is write one word. Lake. We'll write lake on that piece of paper and they'll know where to look for my body."

"But, Zelda—"

"I know, Van AssMan! I know it's impossible, OK? But we have to do it anyway. Just help me."

"OK," Martin said. He moved closer to the desk.

"Alright," Zelda said. "Thank you. Now. We will pick up that pencil. OK?"

"OK," Martin said.

"OK. On three. Ready? One, two, three!" Her spectral hands grasped at the pencil. Martin added his own fingers to the mix. They bumped against Zelda's fingers but didn't have any effect on the pencil whatsoever.

"It's no use," Martin said.

"You're not trying hard enough. Focus!"

"OK," Martin said. He scrunched up his face and envisioned his fingers wrapped solidly around the pencil. Nothing.

"It's not working," he said. "It's not going to work."

"It has to work," Zelda said. "It has to!"

"No," Martin said. "It doesn't."

Zelda collapsed in a heap, tears flowing freely.

Martin took a deep breath and bent down to comfort her. "Look," he said. "Maybe it's better this way."

"Better? How could it be better?"

"Well," Martin said. "Right now, for your family, there's a chance you left of your own accord, a chance you're off doing reckless teenage things right now. A free spirit who might someday come back to them."

"There's also the possibility that I was murdered by some psychopath and my body's rotting away in the woods, being pulled apart by wild animals."

"Yes," Martin said. "I suppose there is. But, the truth, as we both know, is that your bloated corpse is fish food right now in a foul, swampy lake in the middle of nowhere. Do you really want anybody to find it?"

Zelda retched and heaved, but couldn't vomit.

"I think I have my answer," Martin said. "Let's go."

"No," Zelda said. "I can't leave. I can't leave them."

"I know it's hard," Martin said. "But we have to go."

"I need to stay." Zelda's form suddenly shimmered. She faded to a ghostly pale and instead of hovering an inch or so above her bedroom carpet, Zelda's skirts now touched the floor.

"Shit!" Martin said. "Zelda, get up! *Get up!*"

"No. You go, Martin. Please, just leave me."

"Zelda! You're binding yourself to the house!"

"I don't care. I want to stay."

"No," Martin said. "I won't let you! We made a deal!"

He hauled Zelda to her feet and dragged her over to her bedroom wall. She shimmered again and grew even paler.

"Let me go," Zelda said, her voice a faint whisper.

"No." Martin gathered her up in his arms and rushed forward through the bedroom wall. They passed through the side of the house and drifted down toward the lawn, Martin cradling Zelda. Even though she was a ghost, he noted, she wasn't exactly a featherweight. He struggled to keep his grip on her, wishing he'd worked out more during his Earthly life. Zelda pressed her face into his shoulder as he hurried her up her street and out of her neighborhood.

When they came to a park where a few toddlers played under the watchful eyes of their mothers and nannies, he pulled her into an empty gazebo and sat quietly while she slumped on a bench and wept.

When she was done, she sat up and wiped her eyes with the ends of her sleeves. She looked far less pale now and was hovering a respectable inch or so above the gazebo bench.

"I hate you," she said to Martin.

"What's that?" Martin said. "Huh?" He cupped his hand around his ear. "No, no, don't thank me. I only just saved your verloren ass from binding your soul to a house full of people who would piss you off for all eternity."

Zelda was quiet for a minute, mulling over Martin's words.

"Thank you," she finally said. "And I hate you."

"You're welcome," Martin said. "And I can live with that."

Zelda raised an eyebrow at him.

"Er, go on being dead with that. Whatever."

"Whatever," she said.

"So, what do we do now?" Martin asked.

"Isn't it obvious?" Zelda asked.

"Yes," Martin said. "I know. We need to get our souls' new assignments. But how on Earth—or any other plane of existence for that matter—are we going to get back to the Soul Reassignment Office?"

Zelda looked at him as if he'd just been crowned Dumbass of the Year.

"What?" Martin said. "Wasn't that what you were thinking? That we needed to get back to the waiting room?"

"No," Zelda said. "Duh. We need to visit Zeke's house."

Chapter 8

Martin followed Zelda across town, but not without a lot of petulance and whining.

"I really don't see the point of this," he said for the millionth time. "Everyone here has moved on and—as much as we might want to, as much as we might like to…oh, I dunno…slap the half-eaten éclairs out of our loved ones' hands and tell them to wipe the sycophantic smiles off their faces and show some respect for the recently deceased—we can't do anything about it. This whole closure thing? Face it, Zelda: It's not gonna happen for either one of us. And it seems counterproductive, not to mention dangerous, to keep wandering the Earth like this right now. We should focus on getting back to the Soul Reassignment Office."

"But Zeke's family doesn't know what happened," Zelda said. "They're probably wondering where Zeke and I are, wondering whether we're alive or dead."

"Probably," Martin agreed. "But so what? So is your family, and I thought we agreed that we should let them make their own peace with your absence."

Zelda sighed.

"And, in case you've forgotten," Martin went on. "We're ghosts here. Even if we want to tell Zeke's family that he's gone, we can't. Remember?"

"Zeke's family will be different," Zelda said.

"No doubt," Martin mumbled. "I'm sure he comes from a long line of 'different.' A family tree full of screwball leaves."

Zelda stopped and turned to face Martin. "Zeke's mother is a clairvoyant," she said.

"See?" said Martin. "What did I tell you?"

Zelda started moving again. Martin hurried to catch up. "You know that's not a real thing, right?" he said. "Clairvoyants, psychics, mediums. They're all just different names for con artist. You know it's all bullshit, right?"

"Just like ghosts are bullshit?" Zelda countered.

"Touché," Martin said, hanging his head a little and burying his hands in his sweatshirt pocket. "Touché."

They were making their way through a low-rent area. Small, dilapidated houses with piles of junk on the porches lined the street. A stray dog whose ribs showed through its skin ducked down an alleyway between two houses.

"Zeke lived here?" Martin asked.

"So?" Zelda said defensively.

"So nothing," Martin said. "It's just…I guess maybe I can see what he was so pissed off about, you know? Fifty-nine times to Earth and this was the best they could come up with for him in terms of an assignment?"

"Oh, so what?" Zelda said. "You think he should have been born in a mansion? He kills himself over and over again, Martin. I don't think it matters much where they put him."

"Yeah," Martin said. "But, like, they know he's a disgruntled soul, right? That he can't really handle life on Earth? You'd think they'd try to give him a leg up, you know? Save some of these tougher assignments for those seasoned professionals we watched going through the portal back when we were in the waiting room."

Zelda stopped again. "Do you think they take things like that into account?"

"I don't know," Martin said. "I don't know anything." He shook his head. He missed his academic bowl days. He used to be the guy with all the answers.

"Really," Zelda said, looking up and down the street. "Think about it. Do you think you can, like, earn better assignments based on how you do in your last one?"

Martin shrugged.

"I mean, look at us," she said. "We're both pretty new at this, right?"

"As far as we know."

"OK. And we started out somewhere in the middle, right? We were born into middle-class families. We're both average-looking."

"Thank you," Martin said, pretending to preen, running his fingers through his average-at-best brown hair.

Zelda rolled her eyes.

"So, we start out in the middle somewhere and what?" Martin said. "If you complete your mission, fulfill whatever purpose they gave you to fulfill, then you get to come back as a supermodel whose parents own two summer homes and a ski chalet?"

"Maybe," Zelda said.

"Eh," Martin said.

"Eh?"

"Yeah. Eh."

"What is that supposed to mean?"

Wait for It

"I don't know," Martin said. "It's a nice theory and all, I guess. But it's missing something for me. First of all," he said. "If this was my first go-round on Earth, why was I blessed with such extraordinary intelligence? I hadn't done anything to earn it."

Zelda rolled her eyes farther back into her head than probably would have been possible when all the laws of Earthly physics still applied to her body.

"And second of all," Martin said. "Don't you think that the best lessons learned, the biggest changes that can be effected, start with some kind of hardship?"

"And that's why there are things like disabilities?" Zelda asked.

"Maybe," Martin said. "And disease. And poverty."

"Zeke had a learning disability," Zelda said.

"He did?" Martin was surprised.

"He was really smart and everything," Zelda said. "Blessed with extraordinary intelligence, even." Martin flinched. "But he struggled in school, especially when he was younger. He was dyslexic. I mean, can you even imagine what that must have been like for him? Here he is, a guy who remembers learning to read fifty-eight times before, and this time around his brain works a whole different way."

"Huh," Martin said. He didn't think he had ever known anyone with a diagnosed learning disability before. He spent too much time in the honors courses to have ever given that kind of thing much thought. "That must have been tough."

"Well," Zelda said. "Zeke is awesome. He got past it. Learned to compensate or whatever. It turned out to be kind of a non-issue for him in the long run."

They were both quiet for a minute, reflecting on the implications—if any—of Zelda's revelation.

"Come on," Zelda told him, shaking off the unwinnable debate and leading Martin down the street again. Talking about Zeke must have reminded her why they had come to a sketchy neighborhood in the middle of the day.

A few streets over was the house where Zeke had lived. It had once been white, but it was as dingy as all the others on the block now. A side window was boarded up with a sheet of plywood. The porch's requisite junk pile was covered with a blue plastic tarp that flapped open at one corner. A repurposed real estate sign in the yard had been repainted to read:

Miss Nadia
Seer
Fortunes, Healing, Advice

"This was Zeke's house," Zelda said. She looked like she might start to cry again.

"Zelda," Martin said with a sigh. He knew that his verloren self couldn't fatigue, but what was left of his mind was attempting to convince him otherwise. "Zelda, I think we should just go."

"No," she said. "It's OK. I mean, I liked Zeke's mom, but I wasn't super-attached to her or anything. I'll be fine."

"Are you sure?" Martin asked. "Because back at your parents' place—"

"I remember."

"OK. I'm just saying—"

"I know what you're saying."

"Good," Martin said. "Just so we're clear."

"Let's go," Zelda said. She headed along the side of the house and disappeared through the wall. Martin, against his better judgment, followed.

"What the hell?" Zelda shouted.

Martin looked around, trying to get his bearings. He found all the traveling through walls he'd been doing extremely disorienting.

They were in a tiny bedroom furnished with a sagging twin bed and a couple of milk crates stacked as makeshift shelves. A small closet door hung off its hinges, a pile of clothes and other junk spilling out onto the floor. The room was completely devoid of pictures or personal effects.

"Look at this!" Zelda yelled. "Can you believe this shit?" She gestured toward the bed, where a naked man and woman slept, intertwined.

"Uh, no?" Martin said, because he knew that's what Zelda wanted to hear. He tried to look outraged.

"They're in his bed!" Zelda shrieked. "They did it in his bed! Look!"

"Oh," Martin said. He studied the curve of the woman's slender back, let his eyes wander to where a rumpled sheet just covered her bottom.

"Martin!"

"What?"

"You are such a perv!"

"I am not!"

"We have to get them out of here," Zelda said.

"Why?" Martin asked.

"Because this was Zeke's room!" Zelda yelled. "Zeke's bed! Our place to— Oh!" The man stirred and the sheet shifted so that they had way too much of a view. Most of his body was covered in wiry-looking black hair. He scratched himself and rolled over.

"Disgusting!" Zelda lunged toward the bed. "Getupgetupgetup!" she shrieked and tried to jump up and down on the saggy mattress. Of course, she just hovered above it looking absolutely ridiculous.

"Hey, Zelda?" Martin said.

"Yeah?" she looked up, somewhat deflated.

"I think this might be like the Kid Death t-shirt," he said.

Zelda cocked her head to one side. "An important piece of rock-and-roll history?"

"No," Martin said. "Something you just have to let go."

"Right." Zelda sighed. She climbed down from above the bed and started moving toward the bedroom door. Martin followed, relieved. He had been worried he would have to physically remove her from the situation.

Before they reached the door, Zelda darted back toward the sleeping couple and leaned over so her face was right in front of the man's. "You're a shitty brother, Jude Zabar! The shittiest! I just wanted to tell you that! I just wanted you to know!" she shrieked as loudly as she could. The man stirred again, then was still.

"OK," Martin said, pulling Zelda gently by the shoulders. "You told him. He knows it. Let's go."

Zelda was crying.

"It's just a bed," Martin said as they passed through the closed door and found themselves in a short, dark hallway.

"Spoken like a total virgin," Zelda snapped at him. She swiped at her eyes and took off down the hallway.

Martin, cowed, trailed along behind her.

There were voices coming from the front of the house, and Zelda moved toward them.

"Just to be straight, what exactly is our goal here?" Martin asked her. He still felt uneasy about visiting Zeke's house. Something about it felt wrong.

"Just...I just...I just want to give everyone some peace," Zelda said.

"Right," Martin said. "How, exactly?"

"I told you," Zelda said, annoyed. "Nadia's a professional clairvoyant."

"Yes," Martin said. "You mentioned that she conned the desperate and gullible out of their money for a living."

"First of all, screw you," Zelda said, stopping at the end of the hallway and peering out into the main part of the house as if she were afraid of being noticed. "And, second of all, she's the real deal. I think we might be able to communicate with her."

"Well, even if we can," Martin said. "What are we going to tell her, exactly?"

Zelda sighed. "I think you're right that it's better for our families not to find our bodies. Or whatever's left of them." Zelda looked a little sickly. "But, they should know we died. They should know we didn't just run away together and leave them all behind."

"So, just to make sure I'm on the right page here, if Nadia can see and hear me and asks me what's up, I should say…?"

"You should say that Zeke and Zelda passed in a tragic accident and that they miss their families but their souls are at peace."

"So, I should lie?"

"And also say that we were very much in love." Zelda got a little bit of a dreamy look about her and almost swooned on the spot. "That we went on to the next life as soulmates."

"Oh, barf," Martin said because his ghost had nothing in its stomach to actually regurgitate.

"Shut up," Zelda said. "Do you want these people to find peace or not?"

"Not really," Martin said honestly. "No offense or anything, but it's kind of all the same to me."

"Dick."

Martin sighed.

"She's with a client," Zelda said, peering out into the living area again. "We should wait until she's done."

"You say client, I say mark. Tomato, to-mah-to."

"Shut *up*!"

Martin went to slump against the wall, forgetting that he couldn't slump against anything anymore, and lost his balance. He stumbled out into the living room with Zelda right behind him, giving him a look that could kill...were they living. Was he ever going to get used to being a ghost?

A woman who could only have been the seer, Nadia, looked up as they entered the room. She looked around, shook herself a little, and returned her attention to the woman seated before her. Between them was a table covered in a midnight-blue velveteen drape. A row of crystals lying in the center of the table was a nice touch, Martin thought.

Martin hung back and looked around the living room. He could totally see Zelda fitting in there somehow, and Zeke, too, for that matter. Black sheers covered the front window and a lantern with multicolored glass panels hung from the ceiling over the couch, its filtered light adding a touch of otherworldly ambiance to the room. One of the lantern's panels was cracked and the gold-tone chain from which it was suspended was tarnished, giving it a pathetic, backstage prop-y look.

Nadia the Seer wore what had to be a handmade muumuu. Martin was sure there was no way that anyone, anywhere was mass-producing that kind of thing and selling it in any type of retail outlet. The muumuu was also dark-blue velveteen to match her tablecloth, as was the turban that was wrapped around Nadia's head and festooned with several sparkling brooches. Bracelets clanked against each other on both of her arms. Martin didn't feel like he'd walked into the living room of an actual, practicing psychic. Instead, he felt as if he were watching an amalgam of clichés about practicing psychics being forced together on the set of some totally unbelievable television sitcom.

"Now," Nadia said, re-settling her large bottom in a folding chair that didn't look long for this world. "What was I saying, dear?"

"About my aura," an anxious-looking woman in a gray sweatshirt said, leaning over the table and staring intently at

Nadia's crystals. "Some kind of foreign energy in my aura?"

"Yes, yes," Nadia mumbled. "Some negative energy is blocking you. Something…" She looked over her shoulder, staring at the spot where Martin and Zelda stood, frowning. Martin found it unnerving. "Something not of this world," Nadia finished. Her customer sucked in her breath.

"What do I do?" the anxious lady asked.

"Meditate," Nadia said. "Recenter yourself. Re-align your energies. Here." Nadia bent down and rummaged around under the blue velveteen tablecloth. "This should help." She passed a crystal across the table.

"Ooooh, thank you," the woman said, taking the crystal carefully, cradling it in her hands.

"That's forty-five," Nadia said, suddenly business-like. Her customer reached for her purse.

After Nadia the Seer had shown her satisfied—but concerned enough about foreign energies to have scheduled a follow-up reading—customer to the door, she turned and addressed the living room. "Who's there?" she said.

Martin froze. Zelda sucked in her breath.

"Who's there?" Nadia repeated, taking a few steps toward the center of the room. "Spirit," she said, raising her arms dramatically. "Make yourself known to me."

"No," Martin said, backing toward the hallway. "No way."

"Told you," Zelda said with a smirk. She stepped forward and raised her arms the way Nadia had done. "Nadia the Seer," she said in a way-over-the-top dramatic voice. "It is I, Zelda Kozikowski!"

Nadia let her arms fall and closed her eyes. "Spirit who enters my dwelling place, come forward!"

"Ha!" Martin said. "See? She couldn't hear you."

"She senses me," Zelda snapped. She turned to Nadia and intoned, "It is Zelda, the one you called dearheart. I bring news of your son!" in a deep sing-songy voice.

Nadia opened her eyes and stepped toward them. "Rosie?" she whispered. "Rosie, is it you?"

"Oh, shit," Zelda said.

"Who's Rosie?" Martin asked.

Nadia's lip trembled. "Rosie! Sweet Rosie! Have you come back to me?"

"Rosie was Zeke's half-sister. She died a few years ago. She was three." Zelda's eyes were wide, her voice shaky.

"Oh, shit," Martin said.

"She had Down syndrome," Zelda whispered. "There was something wrong with her heart."

"You've got to be kidding me," Martin said.

"Yeah," Zelda snapped. "Zeke's family's been through agonizing grief. Ha ha. Funny joke, huh?"

"Maybe we should go," Martin said.

Nadia was taking a few more shaky steps toward them. "I've been waiting for you," she said. Her voice was husky and Martin could see tears welling up in her eyes.

"No," Zelda said. "Nadia, it's me, Zelda!"

"Rosie!" Nadia said, and fell to her knees, shaking with sobs.

"What do we do?" Zelda asked, frantic.

Martin shrugged. "Leave?" he suggested.

"I really don't like you sometimes," Zelda told him.

Martin sighed.

Zelda rushed forward and hovered near the floor next to Nadia. "We come in peace," she said loudly. "We bring news of Ezekiel. We want you to know that Ezekiel is at peace."

"Child, you torment me," Nadia said between sobs. "Just give Mama a sign!"

"Martin!" Zelda cried. "This is too awful!"

Martin moved forward and crouched down on Nadia's other side. "Zeke is dead!" he yelled loudly, trying to be as dramatic as Nadia and Zelda. "He drowned!"

Zelda gave Martin a nasty look.

"But," Martin said. "Uh. He's happy about it. He's OK, you know?"

"And he's with his one true loooooove," Zelda said loudly in a voice that sounded like a late-movie version of a ghostly moan.

Nadia trembled with emotion. Martin instinctively reached out to put an arm around her, forgetting that he couldn't, and his arm sliced right through the middle of her back. Nadia froze.

"That ain't my Rosie," Nadia said. She stood up. She looked, to Martin, both terrified and terrifying. "What evil spirit is it that comes to torment me with the past?" Nadia bellowed.

"Sorry," Martin said, backing away from the clairvoyant. "I'm not evil, just clumsy."

Nadia didn't seem to have heard him. She strode purposefully over to her table full of crystals, her heavy footfalls making them tinkle against one another. She swept the crystals aside and started pulling other tools of her trade out of a box beneath the table: candles, strange metal objects, stones with what might have been runes carved into them.

"What is she doing?" Martin asked.

"I hope you're happy," Zelda said. "You've totally made things worse."

"Me?" Martin said. "You're the one who made us come here. Look at all the pain you've dredged up for this poor woman."

Zelda looked miserable.

"I'd forgotten about Rosie," she said quietly. "If I'd remembered, maybe I would have just figured it was better for Nadia not to know about Zeke."

"Let's go," Martin said. "Please. Before we make things even worse."

Zelda nodded and took his hand. They moved toward the front wall.

"Stop!" Nadia commanded them. She'd lit some of the candles now, and their flickering flames cast a strange glow around the dimly lit living room. "Evil spirit, cursed soul, you shall trouble me no more!" Nadia poured liquid from a vial into a small bowl on top of her table. She set a bunch of herbs alight and left them to smolder in another dish.

"OK," Martin said. "I've had enough."

"Wait," Zelda said, moving toward Nadia. The seer was sprinkling some kind of granules all over the floor. She curled a length of metal chain into a circle at her feet.

"Evil spirit, dark energy," Nadia intoned. She sprinkled more granules inside the circle. "I call you into my circle."

Zelda drifted forward.

"What are you doing?" Martin asked her.

"It's not me," Zelda murmured. "It's…"

"You hide in cursed darkness, but I call you to the light!" Nadia bellowed. She waved the dish with the smoking herbs around, then set it back on the table. She lifted the dish of liquid up and spilled some into the circle. "I fight water with water!" she yelled.

Zelda moved closer.

Nadia picked up one of her candles and held it over the circle. "And fire with fire!" she said.

Zelda hovered just outside the circle.

"She's ruining her carpet," Martin said disdainfully as candle wax spattered at Nadia's feet.

"I call you from the chaos of the darkness into this blessed circle of light!" Nadia intoned. She was swaying back and forth a little, her eyes half-closed. She seemed to be going into some kind of a trance.

Zelda floated into the middle of the circle.

"Zelda, stop it," Martin said. "Quit fooling around."

Zelda turned to look at Martin, her face full of alarm. "I'm not doing it," she said. "It's—"

Nadia began chanting. Whether she was speaking gibberish or some ancient language Martin had somehow failed to study, he couldn't be sure, but the effect was definitely spooky. To Martin's amazement, the circle of chain began to levitate.

"Uh, Zelda?" Martin said. But Zelda had her eyes closed now, too, and was swaying back and forth to Nadia's rhythmic voice. "Oh, for crying out loud," Martin said. "Zelda!"

Zelda began to spin. The chain Nadia had used to form the circle spun, too, spiraling up Zelda's body.

Martin rushed forward, reaching for Zelda. He found himself unable to reach her, an invisible barrier between them. "Zelda!" he cried.

Nadia's chanting reached a violent crescendo. The flames on her candles leapt up, each one six inches tall. The chain coiled itself around Zelda's waist and she shimmered and shook. Martin could see way too much of Nadia's table through her nearly transparent form.

"Zelda!" he called again futilely.

"Jesus Christ! What the fuck is going on here?" Jude, who'd apparently roused himself from Zeke's bed and put on a pair of sweatpants, strode into the living room, scowling.

Nadia was immediately pulled out of her trance. The candles returned to normal. Zelda became almost opaque again, and the barrier between her and Martin disappeared. Martin seized his chance to rush forward and grab her.

"Are you OK?" he asked. She looked like she might faint.

"You've got to be fucking kidding me right now," Jude said. "I worked all night and all I wanted to do is get a few hours of sleep before my next graveyard shift. But can you keep your stupid magic shit down for five minutes? Oh, no."

"I'm sorry, baby. I—" Nadia seemed suddenly confused and embarrassed, a big transformation from the powerful woman who had been chanting so confidently just a moment before.

"I've really had it with this garbage," Jude said. "The incantations at all hours, the constant parade of losers through the living room." Jude scrunched up his face and used a whiny voice to imitate Nadia's clientele. "How's my aura today, Miss Nadia? What should I do about my cat, Miss Nadia? Is this energy holding me back from getting that job at the beauty shop? Hey, Miss Nadia, does my chakra make me look fat?"

"Jude!" Nadia chided. "Those people put food on our table."

"And look at the rug!" Jude said, gesturing toward the wet, waxy spot Nadia had so recently created. "What the fuck, Ma? What happened to the rug?"

"There was an evil spirit…" Nadia looked down at the mess on the living room floor.

"Well, I should say so," Jude said. "Must have been a real foul piece of shit to come in here and ruin our carpet like that."

"Can we please go now?" Martin said to Zelda. She seemed to have recovered some of her strength.

She nodded weakly.

"Jesus Christ," Jude muttered. "Jesus Tap-Dancing Christ."

Martin and Zelda pushed their way through the wall and found themselves outside once more.

A man in a suit gave them a strange look from across the street, then looked away again quickly. *That's funny,* Martin thought. Nobody in his or Zelda's neighborhood had paid them even half a mind, but every other person in Zeke's 'hood seemed to be some kind of a psychic.

Martin and Zelda glided along the street. Martin had no idea where they were going; he just wanted to get as far away from Nadia and Zeke's old house as possible. Zelda looked completely miserable as they made their way through the neighborhood. Martin couldn't resist making her feel even worse.

"That looks good on you, really," he said sarcastically, pointing to the chain that was still wrapped around Zelda's waist. "Quite a fashion statement. It goes nicely with your whole medieval look there."

"Shut up," Zelda said, tugging tiredly at the chain.

"Seriously," Martin said. "I love it. It's got sort of a heavy-metal, chastity-belt vibe to it. Really hot."

"Shut up!" Zelda pulled and tugged, but the chain didn't budge. "Just help me, would you?"

"Of course, m'lady," Martin said, kneeling down and taking hold of the circle of chain. He tried to slide it down over Zelda's hips, but it was too small. He tried to lift it up, but it wouldn't move past her rib cage. "Huh," he said. "It's stuck."

"Stuck?" Zelda said. "That's impossible."

Martin thought about listing all the impossible things within arm's reach at the moment, but he didn't have the energy. He just gave her an exasperated look that he hoped would suffice.

Zelda struggled with the chain for a little while longer. "Help me!" she said. "Maybe if I can just squish my boobs a little...?" She pulled the chain upward, pulling her stomach in and sucking in her breath.

Martin was more than happy to oblige, but no matter how he pawed at Zelda's body, it was clear that the chain wasn't going anywhere. He inspected it closely. What had once been a simple length of chain coiled on Nadia's floor had magically reformed itself into an unbroken circle at

Zelda's waist, determined to be exactly the right size so as to be impossible to remove. "Amazing," Martin mumbled.

"Alright," Zelda said. "Enough. Get your damned hands off me."

"Aw," Martin said. "You reminded me so much of Zeke just then." As soon as he'd mentioned Zeke's name, Martin regretted it. He saw Zelda flinch a little, then she took off down the street again, Martin flying close behind. Not only was he worried about Zelda, but he also really, really didn't want to be alone in Zeke's neighborhood. Not even as a ghost.

Zelda fled to the bank of a river on the edge of town. It wasn't a grassy recreation area; it was a rocky, litter-strewn spot where a bunch of drainage pipes emptied their contents into the murky water. A factory behind a chain-link fence across the way obliterated any hope of a serene view. It was here that Zelda finally broke down next to the rushing water.

Martin sat down next to her. "I'm sorry," he said.

"We failed!" Zelda sobbed, ignoring his apology. "We totally failed!"

"No, we didn't," Martin tried to tell her. He wasn't used to failing. At anything. Ever. "We got through to Nadia, didn't we? I mean, at least she knew we were there. That's something."

"But we didn't get to tell her about Zeke," Zelda said, still crying. "She doesn't even know that her son is dead."

"Well," Martin said. "She's a clairvoyant, right? Don't you think she knows? Can't she feel it in her, uh, aura or whatever? There weren't any missing-person flyers lying around the Zabar house. Surely she must know, on some level, what's happened?"

Zelda shook her head. "I don't know," she said. She sniffled and wiped her face with her somewhat filthy sleeves. "Honestly, I think they just don't give a shit. You saw Jude. You think he's the type to paper the town with missing-person posters just because his crazy little brother didn't come home? *No!* He's the type to screw some skankly ho bag in his brother's bed."

Martin could see Zelda becoming agitated, ready to scream, but he didn't see a way to head her off.

"Zeke was right all along," Zelda railed. "Don't you see it? Life here sucks! Nobody's happy! Nobody matters! Zeke's been gone for all of what? Five minutes? And his brother's jizz is all over his sheets and his mom's going about her business as usual in the living room. It's like he never existed. It's like he was never even there!"

Zelda flung herself at Martin, who managed to catch her without falling backward. He gave her a little squeeze and she lay her head on his shoulder.

"I just want something—anything—to mean something right now!" she wailed. "People should matter! Our lives should have meaning!"

"Don't freak out on me right now," he begged. "It isn't *all* pointless. You matter, Zelda. You matter to me. Right here, right now, your existence means something to me."

She lifted her head and looked at him.

"You mean something to me, too."

Their faces were very close together. Martin felt Zelda searching his gaze. She leaned a little closer, her lips parted, a question in her eyes.

"Zeke's life mattered, too," Martin said quietly, pulling away from Zelda just a fraction of an inch. "Clearly. His life meant something. To you."

Zelda let go of Martin altogether and swiped angrily at her eyes. "I guess you're right. It did." She shook her head and scowled down at her lap. "But I'm dead, too, now, right? We're all so disposable. Everything around us is, too. You can't take any of it with you. The awesome band t-shirts, the people who totally get you, they're all just left behind."

"One could argue that the impressions these things make on your soul are permanent," Martin tried. "Surely some of your past life experiences will shape what happens to your soul in the course of its next assignment."

"Do you really think so?" Zelda looked at him, considering.

"Sure," Martin said. "Assuming we make it to our next assignments."

"Do you think Zeke has been reassigned already?"

"Maybe." Martin shrugged. "I don't know."

"If he has been, then he's got to be out here somewhere," Zelda said, glancing wistfully up and down the riverbank. "Maybe we should look for him."

"If he's been reassigned already, he's an infant," Martin said.

Zelda sighed miserably. She fiddled with the chain around her waist, lost in thought.

Martin stared at a used condom a few feet away on the riverbank. The physical world really could be vile, he thought. Completely disgusting. A man in a suit appeared to watch them from the chain-link fence around the factory on the other side of the river. Martin figured he was just taking in the crappy view on his lunch break or whatever and wondered how many times, as a human, he himself had taken in the world's scenery and not seen even half of what was really there.

"This sucks," Zelda muttered, rattling her chain. "Do you realize I'm a ghost with a clanking chain? It's too horrible. It's like a cheesy Saturday-morning cartoon."

Martin shrugged.

"Seriously," Zelda went on. "Haven't I been through enough? Why me?"

"Because you believed in her," Martin said.

"What?"

"Nadia. You believed in her clairvoyance. That's why her ritual or whatever it was worked on you. It didn't affect me at all and I was standing right there. I think it's because I'm a skeptic."

"What are you saying?" Zelda looked annoyed.

"Nothing," Martin said. "Not really. You said, 'Why me?' I was just theorizing that it's because you were more gull— Uh, susceptible. Susceptible to the power of suggestion."

"OK," Zelda said. "Because you seem to be some kind of socially awkward special case, I'm going to let you in on a little secret instead of kicking your ass right now. 'Why me?' is almost always rhetorical."

"Ah, I see." Martin smiled. "I didn't mean to insult you, you know. It's not necessarily a bad thing to be so…naive. It's endearing."

"Martin?"

"Yeah?"

"I've already spent way too much of my afterlife telling you to shut up, so can you please just not talk for a little while?"

"Sure," Martin said. He was almost relieved.

Chapter 9

Zelda stretched out along the riverbank and Martin sat next to her.

"I'm so tired," Zelda said.

Martin wanted to argue, to remind her that it wasn't physically possible for her to be tired anymore, but he'd agreed to keep quiet for a while and, true to his word, he held his tongue.

"Martin?"

"Mmm?" He hoped murmuring mmm didn't count as actually talking.

"Why is that man over there staring at us?"

"He's not," Martin said, assuming, since she'd asked him a direct question, that he had permission to speak again. "He can't be."

"But he is."

Martin had been thinking the same thing, but had been trying to convince himself that the man across the river, the man in the suit who was peering at them intently through the factory's chain-link fence, wasn't actually looking at Martin and Zelda. Because, if he were, that would mean he could see them. Which might make him a—

"Demon!" Zelda hissed, sitting up straight.

"He can't be," Martin said. "He's wearing a suit."

Zelda gave him a withering look. She stood up on the riverbank and Martin followed her lead. "I saw a man in a suit watching us outside of Nadia's house, too," Zelda said.

"So did I," Martin admitted.

Zelda took his hand. Martin squeezed. "Run," Zelda said, and they took off.

They left the river behind and headed into a commercial part of town. Zelda was in the lead. Martin kept looking over his shoulder, but there was no sign of anyone pursuing them. They came to a busy intersection with a traffic light.

"Should we hitch a ride?" Zelda asked, looking frantically up and down the street.

"I don't think we can," Martin told her. "See?" He passed through the passenger-side door of a car idling at the light just before it changed. When the car accelerated, it moved on through the intersection—and through Martin, too. He was left there, hovering above the road, as car after car zoomed through his ghostly form. Martin found it a little bit harrowing to have cars flying right through him like that, but it was also kind of an adrenaline rush, too. Or it would have been if he'd still had a properly functioning adrenal gland.

"You've made your point!" Zelda yelled. "Get out of the street."

Martin obliged.

"So, we can't use any kind of a conveyance," Zelda said, looking around. "But I don't think we should just stand here out in the open."

"Where should we go?" Martin said. He wished they'd taken the time to lay out a better plan before they'd snuck through the portal to Earth. "We visited the people we came to visit. We can't help them, they can't see us, and if we go back to them, we could bind our souls….What do we do now?"

"I don't know," Zelda said. "Let's go this way." She floated down the sidewalk. Martin followed.

"To the mall?" he said with disdain when he realized where Zelda was leading him.

"Do you have a better idea?"

"Not to go to the mall?" Martin tried.

"What do you have against the mall?" Zelda sounded personally offended.

"Everything," Martin said. "Where do I start? It's crowded, it's loud, it's full of in-your-face consumerism."

"I know you think you died before your time," Zelda said. "But, let me assure you, you have the soul of an eighty-year-old man."

"Why?" Martin said, flailing his arms in frustration. "Because I hate excess and waste and bad elevator music? Because it gives me the creeps to hang out someplace where people are falling all over themselves to buy made-in-China crap and drink overpriced, over-sweetened coffee-based beverages? Because I can't stand the smell of a thousand bad colognes hovering in a fog at the entrance to every single department store?"

"Look," Zelda said. "If the demons are searching for us, we can't just hang out here arguing and waiting for them."

"Fine," Martin said. "We can duck inside for a little while until we're sure the coast is clear. Then we really need to make a plan. OK, Zelda?"

"OK," Zelda said, and moved toward the mall parking lot. She sniggered to herself. "We'll make sure the coast is clear."

Martin exhaled loudly.

"You really are such a dork sometimes," Zelda said over her shoulder.

"I know," Martin said, shoving his hands deep into the pocket of his sweatshirt. "Thanks so much for reminding me."

Inside, the mall was busy. Holiday decorations were up and SALE signs littered Martin's field of vision. He had to admit that it was a good place to blend in for a little while. Even a demon straight from the foulest pits of Hell would want to avoid the mall at this time of year. Martin instinctively walked toward center court, just the way the mall architects knew he would—that was another thing he hated about the mall, the way it was designed to take away your free will and ability to think for yourself—and sat/hovered on a bench. He gazed toward a gazebo where Santa was greeting a long line of preschoolers. One by one, Santa invited them to sit on his lap and pose for pictures, making them promises he wouldn't have to keep and handing them candy canes. The line snaked around the gazebo twice and at least two-thirds of it was screaming, crying, or hitting someone. Two underpaid elves with acne and prosthetic, pointy ears walked up and down the line, trying to maintain order. While Martin stared in disgust at the Christmas mayhem, a heavyset woman with a cup of coffee waddled over to his bench and sat down right on top of him, passing straight through him and settling herself in his spot.

"For crying out loud," Martin muttered, standing up. He watched the woman take a sip of her expensive, whipped-cream-on-top espresso drink and felt envy clutch at his insides with sharp-clawed hands. It had been so long since he'd had a real cup of coffee.

"Come on," Zelda said. "Let's find somewhere we can think." She glanced at the gazebo. "Those elves are giving me the creeps."

They moved away from the center of the mall, where things got a little quieter, but not less tacky. Lights blinked, snowmen danced, and synthetic snow abounded.

"Want to get a makeover?" Zelda joked as they passed a brightly lit cosmetics store.

"Want to get some clothes designed this century?" Martin snapped as they passed a trendy denim shop.

Zelda looked down at the floor.

"Sorry," Martin said. "The mall makes me cranky. I'm eighty, remember?" They drifted along aimlessly for another minute or two.

"Hey!" Zelda brightened as they passed by the window of a travel agency. "Look!" she said. "Travel! We can go anywhere in the world, Martin. Do you realize that? Italy! Tahiti! Istanbul!" Zelda stared, wide-eyed, at the array of foreign places depicted in the window. "Why don't we plan a trip?"

"Oh, sure," Martin said. "Let's just go on in and book two seats on the next plane to Europe, then sit there on the runway like a couple of asses when it takes off right through us."

Zelda looked annoyed. "We don't need a plane. We can walk. Or float. Whatever. China. Zimbabwe. *Paris!*"

"Zelda," Martin said. "I don't want to float around the world. I think… I think I want to go back."

"Back?"

"Back to the waiting room. Back to a chance at a fresh start."

Zelda didn't say anything.

"I hate this!" Martin yelled. "I can't go on being someone people sit on at the mall much longer."

"I don't think we have a choice," Zelda said. "It's not so bad." She touched Martin's arm.

"Yes, it is!" Martin shrugged off Zelda's touch. "It *is* bad! We shouldn't have come, you know? We shouldn't have snuck through the portal. We were idiots."

"Speak for yourself, Van AssMan. I don't think it's idiotic to want to find some closure, to want to help your family."

"But that's the thing," Martin said with a heavy sigh. "We didn't get any closure. We didn't help anybody. If anything, we probably made Zeke's mom feel worse. Plus, I know for a solid fact that seeing my own parents sure as hell made *me* feel worse."

Zelda rolled her eyes at him.

"What?" Martin said. "You think that's shallow? I don't exactly remember you being all smiles and singsong when we left your house, either." Martin paced up and down in front of the mall travel agency. Posters advertising all the exotic trips he'd never take mocked him through the agency window.

"It's over!" he shouted, flailing his arms wildly at the posters and the mall in general. "All of it! Our relationships, our petty rivalries, our hobbies, our hopes, our dreams. They're all gone. We can't get them back and I don't want to try. I'm done! I'm done being a fucking ghost, Zelda!" He shot another angry look in the direction of the travel agency. "Even if we did go to Zimbabwe right now," he said. "What would be the point?" He held his semi-transparent hand in front of Zelda's face. "We wouldn't even really *be* there! We wouldn't be anyone, anywhere."

"Would you please get a grip?" Zelda looked stern, but she sounded a bit shaken up.

Martin was trying very hard not to cry in front of Zelda. Ghostly basket-case or not, she was still a girl and he didn't want her to see him lose it. He swiped the sleeve of his Honor Society sweatshirt across his face and took a sobering breath.

"I'm sorry for shouting," he said. "I just hate not knowing what to do. And I'm tired—so tired—of being freaked out all the time." His lip trembled. He tried to turn away from Zelda, but she gathered him up in her arms. He sniffled over her shoulder, tried not to let her feel him shaking.

"Martin," she whispered, stiffening in his arms.

"Yeah?"

"The guys in the suits?"

"Yeah?"

"They're here."

Chapter 10

"Run!" Martin said.

"Duh!" Zelda yelled back.

They moved as quickly as they could back the way they came, not stopping to dodge shoppers, signs, or merchandise carts. Martin hated the feeling of all these things flying through his ghost at top speed, but he told himself it was the least of his problems. He looked back over his shoulder as he and Zelda flew through a car on display in the middle of the mall corridor. Two middle-aged men in navy suits were gaining on them, their jackets flapping as they ran. One of them had a bit of a gut that strained against the buttons of his white shirt and the other looked like he hadn't slept in a couple of days, but they were surprisingly fast. They saw Martin glance at them and put on an extra burst of speed.

Martin grabbed Zelda's hand and held on tight. They came to the center of the mall, flew into the middle of the North Pole chaos, both of them looking frantically right and left, trying to find someplace to hide. Elves, glittering snowmen, and wooden reindeer offered no real help.

"Here!" a young man in red called to them. "Over here!"

Martin looked around again, feeling sure the man must be talking to someone else. Someone more visible.

"Stop!" shouted one of the men in navy. His partner seemed to be saying something into a communication device in his hand.

"I'll get you out of here," the man in red said. He was definitely looking right at Martin. "Follow me!"

Martin and Zelda did as they were told, looking over their shoulders every few seconds at the men in hot pursuit. Martin tried not to panic; he focused on trying to keep up with the fast, agile man in the tight red shirt and even tighter red skinny jeans.

Their savior led them down a side corridor and stopped at an open elevator. "Get in!" he yelled. Martin and Zelda rushed past him into the elevator car.

"Shut the door!" Martin shouted. He didn't think he and Zelda would be able to ride the elevator, but hanging out in the shaft might be a good way to avoid their pursuers for a little while.

The man in red stepped into the elevator with them and pressed a button. He swiped some wavy, black hair out of his eyes and raised a dark, perfectly groomed eyebrow at them. "Going down?" he asked with a devastating smile.

Zelda stared at him, entranced.

The elevator started moving and, to Martin's surprise, he and Zelda seemed to be moving with it. He breathed a little sigh of relief.

"Thank you," Martin said. "How—?"

But he realized he didn't need to ask how the man could see them or why he'd offered them his help. Now, without the men in navy on his heels, Martin, proud Honor Society member and former academic bowl champion, was able to figure out the answers all by himself. "Oh, shit," he said. "Oh, big, steaming pile of monkey shit."

Chapter 11

The elevator went down. And down. And down.

Finally, it stopped moving with a little "ding," and the door slid open to reveal a red hallway. Everywhere Martin looked, something red assaulted his sense of sight: red floor tiles, rich red damask wallpaper, wall sconces with ruby glass shades, modern art done in various shades of red in red acrylic frames.

"After you," their handsome escort said, smiling, ushering them out of the elevator. His black eyes sparkled. Martin thought that was a stupid thing for a man's eyes to do. He rolled his own, distinctly unsparkly, plain brown eyes at the man in red as he stepped past him.

"Thank you." Zelda smiled up at the dark, dazzling stranger. She could hardly stop staring at his chiseled features long enough to look around at the red hallway, but when she finally managed to take in her surroundings, her smile faded.

"Where exactly are we?" she asked. "Please say we're in the sub-basement of the mall."

The man, whose tight red jeans and fitted red turtleneck looked right at home in the red hallway, laughed.

"We're in Hell, Zelda," Martin said. "H-E-double-hockey-sticks."

"Double hockey sticks? What are you? Seven, now?"

"Sorry," Martin said. "Sorry if I'm a little freaked out now that we followed a demon straight into the bowels of Hell!"

The man in red laughed again and said, "Please, call me Dmitri."

"Demon?" Zelda frowned at the man who'd lured them into the elevator. "But he's so handsome."

"Do you really think so?" Dmitri asked, leaning toward Zelda ever so slightly. He had a faint Slavic accent that Martin couldn't quite place, which seemed to make him even more alluring to Zelda.

"Oh, yes," she said. "If the escorting-people-to-Hell thing doesn't work out for you in the long run, you know, you could be some kind of a model."

"No," Dmitri the Demon said, waving off Zelda's suggestion with exaggerated modesty. Was he actually blushing a little?

"I'm serious!" she said. She stepped closer to Dmitri and ran a finger along his angular jawline. Her hand trailed down his well-defined pectoral muscles. "Abercrombie, maybe. Or Calvin Klein."

"Cut it out," Martin said, annoyed. He crossed his arms a little self-consciously over his own underdeveloped chest. He narrowed his eyes at the man in red. "Flattery will get her nowhere, I presume?"

"Your friend is right." Dmitri smiled at Zelda. "Come. We must get you checked in." He turned and started down the long red hallway. Zelda drifted dreamily after him. Martin, sighing, brought up the rear.

"So much red," Zelda mused.

"Do you like it?" Dmitri asked flirtatiously.

"Oh, yes," Zelda said happily. "It's gorgeous." She swished her crimson skirts at Dmitri. "Red is totally my color." Clearly, she still hadn't grasped the gravity of their situation.

"We just had it all re-done, you know," Dmitri said. "It used to be completely black, with a huge mural—a re-creation of *Guernica*—all along this one wall here. It was commissioned by my boss and painted by Picasso himself back in the eighties. But, you know, time marches on. We thought it needed an update. The red, it has a nice visual impact, no?"

"Yes," Zelda said. "Huge visual impact."

"Powerful, yes? And slightly terrifying?"

"Definitely," Zelda said. "It's perfect."

"Well, I don't like it," Martin pouted. "Not one bit. And, seriously, who wallpapers over Guernica?" He grabbed hold of Zelda and gave her a little shake, rattling the chain around her waist. "You know who wallpapers over *Guernica*, Zelda?" he shouted, slightly hysterical. "Satan's minions, that's who! Snap out of it, will you. We are royally screwed here!"

They'd come to the end of the hallway. Dmitri opened a frosted-glass door and stepped aside to let them enter.

"This way, my friends," he said, making a sweeping motion with his arm.

"What if I don't want to go?" Martin stared defiantly at their captor.

Dmitri's eyes flashed red and a forked tongue flicked out from between his perfect, unnaturally white teeth. "Then I will make you," he growled in an extremely menacing, entirely inhuman voice.

"Ew," Zelda said, wrinkling up her nose and giving Dmitri a wide berth as she stepped past him and made her way through the door. "Gross."

"Fine," Martin said. God, he was sick of being pushed around all the time. He hoped that in his next life he got to be some kind of popular, sparkly-eyed, muscle-bound super-athlete who called all the shots. Then, he realized that by entering the frosted-glass gates of Hell, he was basically guaranteeing himself zero chance at a next life.

"Fuck," he mumbled as he brushed past the handsome-once-again Dmitri. "This is just fucktacular."

Martin and Zelda found themselves in a bustling office that very closely approximated the DMV in Martin's hometown.

"Welcome to Regional Intake Office #5893. This is our check-in area," Dmitri said proudly. "I'll get you some forms. You'll need to fill them all out in quintuplicate. Blue or black ink only."

"It looks like a DMV in here," Zelda said, validating Martin's opinion of the layout.

"All part of our redesign." Dmitri smiled like a tour guide. "We modeled the whole thing after a notoriously horrible Department of Motor Vehicles office in the Midwest. Same floor plan, furniture, lack of natural lighting, redundant processes that send people from window to window for no real reason at all…"

"It sucks," Martin said, pouting again.

"It really does!" Dmitri looked thrilled. He went over to a nearby counter and picked up two clipboards. "Come," he said, and led Martin and Zelda to a little waiting area. "Sit."

They sat in awful hard plastic chairs.

"This is where I leave you, friends," Dmitri said. "Fill these out." He passed each of them a clipboard with a thick stack of paperwork and a black pen clipped to it. "An escort will be around shortly to collect your forms and walk you through the rest of the process. Do not be delinquent in filling out your paperwork." His eyes glowed menacingly again. Then, he was gone.

Zelda wiggled back and forth in her seat. "Hey," she said. "Did you notice we're not ghosts anymore? Look. I'm sitting!"

"Yeah," Martin said. "I'd noticed." His feet had actually first touched the floor back in the elevator, but his sudden un-ghostliness had been competing with too many other horrible thoughts to make much of an impression on him. "Ghostliness wasn't without its merits, though, right? I mean, what with the imminent torture and all. A little transparency and insubstantiality might have gone a long way where that's concerned."

Zelda sucked in her breath.

"I'm sorry," Martin said. "I shouldn't have brought that up."

Zelda looked down at her clipboard. Her lip was quivering. "I think I'm scared," she said.

"I'm trying to be terrified myself," Martin said. "It's just a little hard with all the fluorescent lighting in here."

"This is all your fault," Zelda accused, finally sounding like she was taking their situation seriously, at least.

"My fault?" Martin said incredulously. "My fault? Sorry, who was it who threw a rubber dagger into the portal back at the Soul Reassignment Office?"

"Well, you were more than happy to go through the door!" Zelda said. "Who followed a freaking *demon* through the mall and right into an evil elevator?"

"Uh, we both did?" Martin said. "We were being chased, remember? I thought Dmitri was part of the whole North Pole thing." Martin suddenly looked sheepish. "He was wearing the same color as the elves."

Zelda looked thoughtful for a minute. "Do you think they were working together?" she asked, putting the blame game on hold. "Dmitri and those guys in the suits?"

"I guess so," Martin said. "Unless…"

"Unless what?"

Martin shifted in his seat, tapped his clipboard uncomfortably. "Unless the suits were Seekers."

"Seekers?"

"Yeah," Martin said. "Remember the manual said the soul-reassignment place sends Seekers to round up the verloren and bring them back to the office? Wait. I think I still have my copy." Martin reached into the kangaroo pocket in the front of his Honor Society sweatshirt and pulled out the little book.

"Nerd," Zelda said, dismissing the manual with a wave of her hand. "But you might be right. I don't see those other guys down here."

Martin put the book away and nodded.

"Maybe we should have gone with them," Zelda said.

"The path not taken…" Martin mumbled.

"I never intended for any of this to happen, you know. I just meant to bring some peace and comfort to our souls and our families."

"Well," Martin said. "We all know what the road to hell is paved with. Figuratively, of course. In reality, it was some kind of garish red floor tiling, wasn't it?"

"What are we going to do?" Zelda asked. She twisted some of her red skirting in her hands.

Martin glanced up at the long counter where lots of handsome men—and a few beautiful women—in red jackets and ties looked extremely busy. He and Zelda were the only two in their section of the waiting area, but down the line, he saw several other souls hunched over clipboards in their laps, perplexed expressions on their faces. Some of them were very old, some were very young, and some were somewhere in the middle. Some of them looked scared, some of them seemed sad, some of them were managing to keep stone faces. But all of them were filling out their forms.

"I guess we'd better start filling out our paperwork," Martin said. "What else can we do?" He pulled the pen off his clipboard and stared at it. "Well, I'll be darned," he said. "I guess it's official." He held the pen out for Zelda to inspect. The black ballpoint was engraved with shiny red lettering: Property of Satan.

Chapter 12

Name:

Martin Van Assen

Question 1:

Reason for birth?_____

Question 2:

Where, exactly, did it all go wrong?_____

Question 3:

On a scale of 1 to 10, how repentant are you with regard to your past misdeeds?_____

Oh, here we go again with the bullshit questions, Martin thought. He was really annoyed that he hadn't been able to properly complete even one assignment in his entire afterlife so far. Not one.

He peeked at the clipboard in Zelda's lap. She'd filled in her name, then started doodling daisies in the margins of her paper. The sight of them made Martin smile. He peeked ahead at the rest of his forms. Dmitri hadn't been kidding about the office's affinity for redundancy. There were five copies of each form on his clipboard and none of them looked any easier to complete than the first one. It was the expected brevity of the answers, Martin decided, that was throwing him off. He'd always favored essay questions himself. You could slip so much extraneous information into the answer. Even if you didn't know the exact response your examiner was looking for, you could pretty much partial-credit your way out of trouble.

There were no essay questions in the paperwork from Hell.

Martin just knew he was going to hate it there.

"Is it hot in here?" Zelda asked, fanning herself with her clipboard.

It had been a while since Martin had been able to perceive temperature, as his ghostly form had been immune to hot and cold. But, yes, now that Zelda mentioned it, he was a little warm. He pulled at his collar. "You know," he said. "I think it is."

"I've always hated the heat," Zelda remarked.

"Everybody hates the heat," Martin said. "That's probably why it's hot here."

"What do you think they're going to do to us?" Zelda asked quietly.

"I have no idea," Martin said. "I've been wondering the same thing."

"Do you think they'll let us stay together?"

"I don't know." Martin hadn't considered being separated from Zelda. He'd only known her since that fateful day he'd hit his head on the movie-theater urinal, but he already couldn't imagine his afterlife without her. He reached out and took her hand. "Whatever happens," he said. "I want you to know that I'm glad we got to know each other."

"Me, too," Zelda breathed. She leaned in close to Martin, closing her eyes demurely, waiting, waiting for him to close the gap between them.

Martin leaned in, too, over the arm of his plastic waiting-room chair and touched his lips gently to hers.

"Hell-fucking-lo!"

Martin and Zelda sprang apart, embarrassed and breathing a little heavily.

"Zeke!" Zelda squealed, and jumped out of her seat. She hurled herself at Zeke, who was looking uncharacteristically sharp in a jacket and tie. He caught her up in his long arms and held her tight.

"You're still dead!" Zelda shouted happily. "Thank God! I had no idea what had happened to you! I thought you might have been alive again already!"

Zeke kissed Zelda fondly on the head and ran his hands over her body. "Nope," he said. "Still deceased." He rubbed her back and leaned in to kiss her on the lips.

Martin thought he might barf.

"Nice hardware," Zeke said, pulling away from Zelda with a smile when his fingers found the chain around her waist. "Did you go visit my mother by any chance?"

"Yes," Zelda said. "We were trying to reassure her—our families have no idea what happened to the two of us—and she put some kind of a spell on me."

"An evil-spirit bind," Zeke said, nodding. "She used to do them all the time when we were little. She always thought evil spirits were tormenting her. Mostly, it was just me and Jude, though." Zeke laughed. "This is probably the first time her spell's ever worked. She must have been thrilled." Zeke smiled, then frowned. "It's probably also the reason you're here. We get a lot of souls on the run who were bound by voodoo priestesses or amateur exorcists right before the demons got them. I think the bind makes souls easier to track or something."

"Well, can you get it off me?" Zelda said. "It's such a cliché."

Zeke slipped his hand inside the chain and used it to pull Zelda close. "I might know the chant to release it," he said. "But I don't know if I want to. It's pretty sexy in a fifty-shades-of-medieval-bondage sort of way."

Zelda giggled.

"That's what I told her," Martin said.

Zeke frowned and looked over Zelda's shoulder at Martin. "Are you still here, Van AssMan?" he said.

Martin sighed. Of course his own personal Hell would have to include Zeke Zabar. Of course it would.

"Alright," Zeke said, turning his attention back to Zelda and her chain. He grasped the metal in his hands and closed his eyes. He furrowed his brow and said a few words that sounded like the mysterious language Nadia had been speaking back at her house. In a few moments, the chain came apart and Zelda was free.

"My hero!" she cried and flung herself back into Zeke's arms. He tossed the chain to the floor of the waiting area, where it landed with a clatter and then slowly began to glow. Strange white flames grew up around it and the chain incinerated itself, link by link, until there was no trace of the metal left behind.

Zelda kissed Zeke on the neck and lay her head on his shoulder contentedly.

"So, you're one of them?" Martin said to Zeke, jerking his head toward the long row of clerks behind the counter. He stepped forward and flapped the lapel of Zeke's red jacket disrespectfully. "Nice threads."

Zeke didn't seem to take offense. "I know, right?" he said. He looked almost proud of himself. "I never saw myself as the functionary type when I was alive," he admitted. "But this is actually a pretty sweet gig. And," he said, concern furrowing his brow. "Working in the office here sure beats where you're going." He put an arm around Zelda and pulled her close.

"Where we're going?" Martin said. He swallowed hard and tugged at the neck of his sweatshirt.

"Down," Zeke told him.

"Down?"

"Several levels down, actually." Zeke looked more and more worried as he squeezed Zelda. "There are a bunch more clerical offices on the floors below us; you'll have to go through all the usual intake procedures, but then, yeah." Zeke took a small electronic-looking device out of his pocket and frowned at it. "Yup, it's right here. You guys are slated to go all the way down."

"But why?" Zelda said. "We didn't do anything wrong."

Martin shot her a look.

"We didn't do anything too terribly wrong," she amended. "Not by today's standards. Not on purpose. Not really."

"Look," Zeke said. "I don't make the rules. You guys were caught wandering the Earth as lost souls. You were fair game. And, frankly, with all the additions they've been putting on around here and the big redecorating efforts, I think the boss man's been itching for some bigger numbers lately. They've really stepped up their recruiting efforts."

"So how come you didn't go 'all the way down?'" Martin asked. He narrowed his eyes at Zeke.

Zeke shrugged. "I guess I was supposed to," he said. "They picked me up right after I split from you guys, actually. That night, I drifted into a bar, looking for some kind of a good time, I guess. I don't know. I was pretty pissed off, right? And as soon as I got there, I noticed all these freakishly good-looking dudes in tight red pants. At first I was all like, 'Oh, shit, I've stumbled onto some kind of red-pants-fetish scene.' Then, I realized they could all see me. One of them made me an offer I couldn't refuse, and before I knew it, I wound up here."

"What was the offer?" Martin asked. "The one you couldn't refuse?"

"A drink, of course," Zeke answered. "He said he'd buy me a drink."

"Was it Dmitri?" Zelda asked. She looked a little dreamy as she uttered his name. "That's who brought us here. He found us in the mall."

"I never caught his name," Zeke said, shaking his head. "There are, seriously, millions of those guys, and they all look kind of alike. I don't even know if they have real names," he said. "I think they just tell people whatever they want to hear. They're trouble, Zel." Zeke sounded worried. "Really. Stay away from Dmitri or whatever he calls himself, OK?"

"Sure," she said, but she sighed and looked off into space.

"So, they picked you up at a bar," Martin said. "Which is stupid because you should have realized you couldn't drink anything as a freaking ghost. But, then what? They just shook your hand and handed you a red blazer and said, 'Welcome to the team?'"

"Not exactly," Zeke said. He looked mildly uncomfortable. "I was sitting right here at first," he said, indicating the waiting area around them. "Filling out my paperwork, being pissed off about everything, wondering what happened to you guys." He gave Zelda a little squeeze. "Then, a few windows over, I had to sit for a photo so they could print out my picture ID."

Martin raised an eyebrow.

"I know, right?" Zeke said. "But I shit you not." He dug a plastic card out of his pocket and held it out for Martin and Zelda to inspect.

"You look hot, babe." Zelda smiled.

"Thanks," Zeke said, and winked at her.

"So, what?" Martin said. "You turned out to be somewhat photogenic and they started grooming you for the role of demon?"

"No," Zeke said. "Nothing like that. The computer froze right after the girl at the photo counter snapped my picture and it wouldn't print out my ID. She tried rebooting it, like, three times. No dice. I offered to step behind the counter, see what was what. I got the thing back up and running again in a few minutes flat. She was super-grateful." Zeke turned as red as his blazer and tugged at his collar a little. "Like, really grateful. You know. Anyway, next thing I know, I'm one of them."

"So, you're, like, their tech-support guy?" Martin asked.

"Oh my God!" Zelda said, fuming. "I can't believe this. I can *not* fucking believe this! Zeke Zabar, you banged that picture-counter girl!"

"What?" Martin said. Had he missed something?

"Zel, listen—"

"No! You listen! Martin and I were out wandering the Earth, trying to tell your family that you were dead, getting spirit-bound by your crazy mother, being chased by weird dudes in suits, accidentally following a demon, and you were just hanging out here the whole time, banging some whore from Hell!"

"She isn't a whore," Zeke said, trying to maintain his composure. "She's actually a really nice person."

"A really nice person from Hell?" Martin said. "Holy oxymoron, Batman!"

Zeke ignored him. "We were broken up," he said to Zelda. "You broke up with me, remember? And we were all verloren! I didn't think I'd ever see you again."

Zelda was so furious her whole body trembled. "I can't believe I ever loved you," she said.

"Zel—"

"Don't talk to me!" Zelda pushed him away. "You know, I think I can smell her on you. You disgust me!" Zelda stepped away from the waiting-area chairs and addressed the line of red jackets working behind the counter. "I'm ready to go!" she shouted. "I'd like to get on down to the depths of Hell now, please!" The people behind the counter looked at her suspiciously, then frowned and went back to their work.

"Zel, cut it out," Zeke said. "Seriously. Shh."

"Don't you shush me, you dirty, stupid man-whore," Zelda said, but Martin noticed that she did lower her voice a bit.

"Look," Zeke said. "You've been sucking face with Van AssMan this whole time, haven't you?"

"No," Zelda said, looking down.

Martin tried not to take offense.

"I saw you!" Zeke said. "*Twice!*"

Zelda let her breath out in a huff.

"It doesn't matter, OK?" Zeke said. "None of it matters."

"Oh, that's what you'd like me to think, isn't it?" Zelda hissed. "That's like, your mantra, right? 'Nothing matters, it's all meaningless, everything is bullshit.' Well, fuck you, Zeke. Because some things matter. They just do."

"That's not what I meant." Zeke sighed and ran his hand through his hair. Martin almost felt sorry for him for a second. Almost. "I just meant that who did what with whom is beside the point right now. We have to find a way to get you guys out of here before they send you downstairs."

"You can do that?" Martin asked.

"I don't know," Zeke said. "Maybe I can pull a few strings."

"If you mean maybe you can fuck a few fiendish secretaries, don't bother," Zelda said. "We're not interested."

"Speak for yourself," Martin said. "Zeke, seriously. Do what you've gotta do, man. I'm definitely interested."

"Just sit tight," Zeke said. "Both of you. Keep a low profile. Fill out your forms like good little damned souls, alright? Luckily, I was able to get myself assigned to your case. I'm supposed to escort you through the bureaucratic process here. Let me scout around a little bit, see what I can do, clear my schedule for a little while. I'll be back." He looked at Zelda like he wanted to say something else, but she didn't meet his gaze.

"Thanks," Martin said.

"Don't thank me yet," Zeke told him.

"Hey, Zeke?" Martin said.

"Yeah?"

"I don't suppose there's any coffee around here, is there? Since we have to wait and all. One of those crappy hot beverage machines? A cup of instant? Anything?"

"Oh, yeah, sure," Zeke said. "What do you want? Latte? Cappuccino? I can just nip over to the espresso bar for you."

"You have an espresso bar down here?" Martin's eyes got big and his mouth watered.

"No," Zeke said flatly. He turned on his heel and walked away.

As soon as Zeke left, Zelda began to tremble with rage all over again.

"Can you believe him?" she shrieked, looking to Martin for support.

"Actually, I can," Martin said, and went to sit a few chairs away from her. He didn't want to talk about Zeke Zabar or his hook-ups in Hell. He felt they both had bigger problems at the moment. He frowned determinedly at his clipboard again.

Zelda stomped her foot in frustration and hurled herself to the floor, pounding her fist on one of the waiting room chairs. *Way to keep a low profile,* Martin thought, but he didn't look up from his paperwork.

Chapter 13

Zeke returned a while later, long after Martin had managed to fudge his way through his ridiculous, repetitive forms. His hard plastic chair was so hellishly uncomfortable that he was actually relieved to see the crazy-eyed Zeke roll up, looking a little crazier-eyed than usual and pulling nervously at his collar.

"OK, you two," Zeke said, all official-like. "Get your paperwork together and let's go." Zeke looked from side to side and straightened his already-straight tie. Martin knew that he himself wasn't exactly an ice cube under pressure, but he thought that if Zeke didn't cool it, he was going to get them all busted.

Martin stood up and handed Zeke his clipboard. "I think you'll find that everything's in order," he said. "Sir," he added, maybe a tad too loudly.

"Great," Zeke said, nodding an overly official nod. "And you? Miss? Your paperwork?"

"Fuck you," Zelda said. She still sat on the floor. Her clipboard was untouched.

"Jesus!" Zeke said angrily. Another passing functionary stopped in his tracks and gasped. "Sorry," Zeke said. "Sorry! I meant, 'Oh fuck!'" Zeke's co-worker shook his head in disapproval and hurried away. Zeke tugged uncomfortably at his tie again and picked up Zelda's clipboard. He flipped through her forms frantically. "Seriously, Zel?" he said, sounding panicked. "Not a single question?"

Zelda sulked.

"Damn it," Zeke said. He grabbed a Property of Satan pen and started scribbling answers as fast as he could.

Martin was annoyed. He'd probably spent hours on his forms. "Do you seriously just know all these answers off the top of your head?" he couldn't help asking.

"No," Zeke admitted with a snort. "I'm just making shit up. It doesn't matter anyway. They're just going to give you new forms with pretty much the same questions on them at the next window." He wrote furiously, glancing at his watch between questions.

"For real?" Martin said. "We have to do this all over again? That's..."

"Hellish. I know. That's kind of the point." Zeke finished his work with a flourish and stood up. "Come on, you guys," he said, looking around the office again. "Let's go. Window Two. Move it."

Zelda remained on the floor.

Zeke squatted down in front of her. "Zelda," he said. "At this minute, nothing would give me greater pleasure than to damn you to Hell for all eternity. However." Zeke cleared his throat and pulled at his collar again. "I'm sure that, if that were to happen, we'd both cool off in a few days and regret it. You more than me, I'm betting, since I'd still be up here in the relatively pleasant intake office and you'd be down below with the torture chambers and the eternal flames and whatnot. Do you understand me?"

Zelda didn't answer.

"So," Zeke said, trying to control his temper and, for the most part, succeeding. Only his eyes flashed with fury. "What I need you to do right now is stand up and follow me to Window Two. If you don't, one of my superiors will deem you a problem case and relieve me of my duties as your escort. Your descent will be expedited and I will have no chance to bail you out. Got it? Now, get up."

Martin held his breath. He was sure that Zelda was going to continue to slump on the floor, inert, but to his great relief, she stirred and got to her feet. She held her head up tall and looked Zeke right in the eye.

"That's better," Zeke said.

Zelda spit in his face.

Zeke wiped her saliva off his cheek with his hand and turned away from her. "Follow me," he said coolly.

He led them just a couple rows of waiting-room chairs over, where they queued up in front of Window Two. There were only a few damned souls and their escorts ahead of them in line, but Martin got the sense from everyone's posture that their wait there had already been rather long.

Martin rolled up the sleeves of his Honor Society sweatshirt. If he'd had anything on underneath it besides a ratty old undershirt, he'd have taken the bulky thing off. He couldn't exactly say he was suffering from Hell's heat (not yet, anyway), but he was uncomfortably warm. Martin decided that this feeling was almost worse—and definitely more annoying—than being completely overcome by an inferno. Beside him, Zelda fanned herself uselessly with her hand. The futility of the gesture irritated the already-on-edge Martin. In keeping with the plan to maintain a low profile, though, he didn't comment on it for fear of starting an argument.

The man immediately in front of them in line was an older gentleman, in his late sixties maybe, with just a horseshoe of white hair left on the back of his head. His silver-framed glasses were bent out of shape and he wore what looked like a prison jumpsuit: a beige button-down one-piece with a black number printed across the back. Tears ran silently down his weathered cheeks, but he held his head up high and clasped his hands in front of himself, too proud to completely break down, yet not entirely accepting of his fate. Martin thought he knew how he felt.

"What a bunch of assholes we've had through here today, huh?" the older man's escort said to Zeke. "Look at this guy here." He gestured to the man he was accompanying. "Adultery. Money laundering. Murder for hire. Kidnapping and assault. Total piece of shit." The old man stoically refused to acknowledge his escort's comments.

"Yeah," Zeke said. "Wow."

"What've you got here?" the other escort asked him. "A twofer, huh? Some kind of Bonnie and Clyde deal?"

"Nah," Zeke said, a half-smile tugging at the corner of his mouth. "Nothing that cool." He gestured toward Zelda. "She's a big old prostitute," he said. "Really nasty business. Turning underage tricks in the back of the school bus. Catered to nerds with wench fantasies, obviously." Zeke made a sweeping motion along the length of Zelda's corset top. "And this guy." Zeke pointed to Martin. "He basically masturbated himself to death watching animal husbandry videos."

"Huh," the other escort said, looking at Martin and Zelda and shaking his head. "What a couple of sickos."

"Tell me about it," Zeke said. Martin could see that he was trying not to laugh. Martin, for his part, was trying not to kick Zeke's ass. Zelda's face was bright red and she looked like she was trying not to scream. Martin could see that it was taking everything the three of them had to keep quiet and stare straight ahead.

When they finally reached the woman behind the counter at Window Two, Zeke handed over their paperwork and Martin and Zelda were each given a whole new batch of forms to fill out in quintuplicate. Zeke had been right: the questions seemed awfully repetitive.

"Follow me," Zeke said to them as they left the window, clipboards in hand.

"Was that really necessary?" Martin asked as evenly as he could, trying not to fume. Zelda was fuming enough for all of them at the moment. "Animal husbandry videos?"

Zeke chuckled. "Sorry," he said. He looked at Zelda when he said it and Martin tried not to mind. "I couldn't resist."

"Well, next time, try," Martin said.

"Seriously, guys, we're going to have to make every effort to seem like just another escort leading just another couple of sinners through the intake process. OK? We escorts are the lowest of the low around here, the bottom of the food chain. If anyone suspects me of anything funny, we'll all be on the express elevator to the basement. The escorts always rag on the incoming souls. Being too nice to them is actually frowned upon for obvious reasons. I was just trying to keep up appearances. You guys try to do the same."

Martin and Zelda followed Zeke to another section of plastic chairs, and Martin sat right down and got to work. He really wanted to get all the formalities over with. He was anxious to get to the part where Zeke busted them out of there.

Zelda, too, took her clipboard and headed for a seat a few chairs down from Martin. Martin noticed that she stomped on Zeke's foot as she made her way past him, but at least she sat down and started writing. Martin was glad she seemed to be coming around. He didn't want her tiff with Zeke to ruin their chances of escape. Zeke looked a little more relaxed as Zelda appeared to get with the form-filling-out program.

"Alright," Zeke said. "I'll be back in a little bit. Um...I'm supposed to tell you to enjoy some television while I'm gone." Zeke gestured to a small flat screen sitting on a side table.

"Don't do us any favors," Zelda snapped.

"I'm not," Zeke said. "Believe me." He sighed and pushed a button on the TV. He looked at Zelda again. "I really am sorry," he said. When nobody said they forgave him, he sighed and left.

Instead of showing CNN, a talk show, or other typical waiting-room fare as Martin had expected, the TV appeared to be part of a closed-circuit camera system. Martin stopped his paperwork long enough to lean forward and frown at the screen. He seemed to be looking at the interior of a huge stone chamber. Medieval-looking torches lined the walls, a huge well of some kind stood in the middle of the floor, and a cart full of rusty-looking tools stood next to it. "Hey," Martin said. "Is that...?"

"IT IS," appeared on the TV screen in bold white lettering.

"Zelda," he said. She was looking at her clipboard. "Zelda!"

"Shut up," she mumbled.

"Zelda, look! Downstairs! I think…I think it's a live video feed from Hell."

Zelda sat up and looked.

"LIVE VIDEO FEED FROM HELL," scrolled across the screen.

"It doesn't look so bad," Zelda said, shrugging and going back to her forms. "Zeke's just probably trying to freak us out with all his 'torture chambers and eternal flames' bullshit."

"Yeah," Martin said. "Maybe."

"MAYBE NOT," the television said.

A group of super-handsome demons in red came into view, and Zelda looked up again. "Do you see Dmitri?" she asked.

"I see fifty Dmitris," Martin muttered.

Behind the demons came a group of ordinary-looking people, damned souls like Martin and Zelda, Martin presumed. They milled about nervously, sticking close to one another. It looked like an unpleasant adventure, Martin thought, but not as horrible as he'd expected.

Then, all hell broke loose.

The demons shed their handsome skins and trendy red outfits and grew to about three times their usual size. Black, shiny skin covered every inch of their naked, muscled forms.

"Whoa!" Zelda said, leaning forward in her chair. "Look at their huge—"

"No," Martin said. "Grow up." The demons were what one might call well-endowed.

Cloven hooves replaced the demons' feet and their hands were long and tapered, ending in thick, black claws. Their faces, once smooth and perfect, wrinkled into black masks. Their noses retracted into their skulls, their mouths widened to show rows of pointy teeth and hideous forked tongues. Their eyes became narrow slits with bright red irises that looked like burning coals set into their heads.

The souls of the damned, understandably, appeared to be screaming hysterically and clutched at one another, looking for an exit and finding the room completely sealed. The demons appeared to enjoy the effect their transformation was having, though the expressions on their faces couldn't have been described as anything even close to smiles. A few of them opened their mouths and spit fire at the crowd.

One demon moved over to the cart full of tools and grabbed an ancient-looking forceps. He pulled a man from the crowd, lifted him up with one hand, and used the forceps to reach into his mouth and rip out his tongue. In case Martin missed it, which he hadn't, the demon dropped the twitching, tongueless man to the ground, and started extracting the tongue of the next.

"THESE ARE THE LIARS," the television informed him.

Meanwhile, a few other demons started setting people on fire. They stared at the damned with their red-hot-coal eyes until their victims began to writhe in agony, flames shooting out of their various orifices, burning, it appeared, from the inside out.

"Holy shit," Martin said.

Zelda whimpered.

"THESE ARE THE IMPURE," the TV read.

Yet other demons had started grabbing people by their feet and dangling them head-first into the well, where a substance that was definitely not water bubbled up to the surface and churned a smoldering red. The dangling souls thrashed about as the demons held their heads below the surface.

"Lava?" Martin wondered out loud.

"Turn it off!" Zelda cried, clutching at her throat and gasping for air. She clearly remembered her own drowning experience all too well, and could no longer watch. She hid her face in her hands.

Martin stood up and tried pushing buttons on the TV but, of course, he couldn't turn the video feed off. He didn't want to watch anymore, but he couldn't look away, either. Everyone was being tortured in different ways, then hung from hooks on the wall. Once the whole group was suspended from the giant meat hooks, the demons spun in gleeful circles, filling the entire room with their supernatural fire. There was no sound on the television, but Martin could plainly see the agony in the victims' contorted faces.

"Enjoying the show?" Zeke asked grimly, coming up behind Martin and reaching past him to turn off the television.

"No," Martin said. "We're not."

"I really am sorry about that," Zeke said. He ran his hand through his hair and looked at Zelda, whose face was still buried in her hands. "I swear I took it easy on you guys. That was Chamber One. You wouldn't believe the shit that's going on in Chamber Twenty-Three today." Zeke shuddered. He looked at Martin and Zelda. "OK, guys," he said. "Grab your clipboards, please. Let's go. Window Three. Chop chop."

Martin picked up his clipboard and tried to shake off what he'd seen on the monitor. "Listen," he said. "I'm all for jumping through these bureaucratic hoops." He held up his clipboard. "But at what point do we get to hurdle some of this red tape and get the fuck out of here?"

"Shh," Zeke said. "Keep it down, alright? I have a plan."

"You do?"

"Yeah." Zeke looked at Zelda uncertainly. She still sat with her face covered. She might have been crying a little. "But the plan will only work if we make it off this floor without incident." Zeke went and crouched in front of Zelda's chair. "Zel?" he said quietly. "Come on. I'm gonna try to get you out of here, but you've got to work with me a little. OK?"

Zelda looked up at him, sniffling. "Oh, Zeke," she said. "It was so awful."

"I know," he said. He reached out and hugged her, then let her go and looked around to make sure none of his peers were watching. "Come on," he said gently, taking her hand and pulling her to her feet. "It's going to be OK."

Martin watched the two of them jealously, simultaneously envying both Zelda's indefatigable affection for Zeke and his attempts to comfort her. Martin wished somebody would hold *his* hand and tell him everything was going to be OK. He'd had to watch the gruesome torture channel, too, after all. He'd been through just as much as Zelda had; his soul was in just as much peril as hers.

Zeke retrieved Zelda's half-finished paperwork, jotted answers on the blank lines, and led her to the next queue. Martin followed a little sullenly, filling in the rest of his own forms as he went. "So, this plan of yours," he said to Zeke, looking up from his paperwork. "It's a good one?"

"I never said that," Zeke told him.

"But it's been done before, right?" Martin said, determined now that someone would say something at least a little bit reassuring to him. "I bet that in a bureaucracy this large, souls slip through the cracks all the time. As many people bust out as make it all the way downstairs, right?"

"I don't think so," Zeke said, double-checking Zelda's forms. He looked up at Martin. "I'm pretty sure they haven't lost anyone yet."

"Awesome," Martin said flatly. The line inched forward. "Just awesome."

Zeke ushered Martin and Zelda to several more windows where they were asked to fill out more and more paperwork of an increasingly inane variety. Window Three demanded a list of reasons for their damnation, offering them page after page of suggestions with tiny checkboxes next to them. "Be sure to check all that apply," the clerk had informed them.

"What to pick, what to pick?" Martin mumbled. "Idolatry? Blasphemy? False prophecy? Oooh! There's an 'other' option. Maybe I can write in, 'clerical error.'"

Zeke shook his head with an air of superiority. "Almost everybody writes in clerical error. They're just going to make you go back and fill it out all over again."

"So, what am I supposed to check?" Martin said.

Zeke grabbed his clipboard, made a few marks, and passed it back.

"Hubris?" Martin said. "Covetousness? Self-abuse? Boasting? Lusting? Foolishness? Foolishness! Thanks a lot."

"Don't mention it," Zeke said.

The forms from Window Four seemed to be some kind of long, twisted Rorschach test where Martin was supposed to write down his reactions to different hellish images.

"Market research," Zeke noted when Martin questioned the forms' relevance. "You know. They gather data about what freaks people out the most and adjust their décor and methods accordingly."

"Right." Martin nodded. "How strategic."

Window Five passed them forms regarding their most heart-wrenching Earthly experiences. "Lie on question fifty-seven," Zeke advised them. "They use that answer to inform the torturous hallucinations they induce in solitary confinement."

"But," Martin said. "If we're not going all the way down, it shouldn't matter, right?"

"Lie anyway," Zeke said, looking him right in the eye. "Just in case."

By the time they collected their paperwork from Window Seven, Martin was just plain fed up with forms. "Find at least 500 anagrams of the word 'brimstone' and group them by number of letters? List the first 300 four-digit prime numbers? What the fuck is this?"

Zeke smiled. "This one's pretty much just busywork," he admitted. "If you need any help with the answers there, Academic Bowl Champ, don't be too proud to ask."

"No, thank you," Martin said smugly.

"OK," Zeke said with a smirk before he took off again. "Let me know if you change your mind when you get to the crossword puzzle on page thirty-eight. It's a doozy."

"You know what's the worst?" Zelda mused, looking up from her paperwork to gaze after Zeke.

"Being in Hell?" Martin guessed, frowning at his clipboard.

"No. I mean, well, *yeah*. But besides that? What really pisses me off is that we'll never know what could have been, you know? I mean, maybe I would have invented a whole new multi-sensory video gaming experience or married Zeke at a drive-through chapel in Las Vegas and had six curly-haired kids."

"Maybe you're better off not knowing," Martin said, crossing out his answer to question 1,568 in frustration.

"Maybe," Zelda said, chewing on the end of her Property of Satan pen. "But it bothers me. I mean, I'll never know whether my family finds out the truth about what happened to me. I'll never know whether or not Jenny treats my Kid Death shirt with the respect it deserves or winds up using it as a car-washing rag." Zelda sounded close to tears again.

Martin put down his pen and looked at her.

"Listen," he said. "Nobody hates not knowing things more than I do, OK? When we first got to the Soul Reassignment Office, all I could think about was whether or not my parents missed me and what was going to happen with the academic bowl team. Do they win without me? Go down in flames? Wear black armbands in my memory?" Martin couldn't help looking a little wistful at the prospect of his long-time rival, Brandon Woo, forced into public mourning for him. "But now? Here?" Martin gestured around Hell's intake office. "I'm starting to think Zeke was right. The stuff that seemed so important back on Earth? None of it really matters. Not anymore. Not when we're facing eternal damnation. Maybe it doesn't matter what you have on Earth or how people remember you when you're gone as much as it matters that you appreciate it all while you're alive. And maybe—just maybe—it really doesn't matter all that much in the grand scheme of things who wins what nerd bowl trophy."

Zelda stopped chewing on her pen and looked at Martin. "I sincerely hope," she said. "That you aren't equating whether or not your former teammates win a plastic nerd bowl trophy with the uncertain fate of my one-of-a-kind, totally irreplaceable Kid Death t-shirt."

"Of course not," Martin said with a sigh and a small smile. "I wouldn't dream of it."

He went back to his paperwork.

Chapter 14

After what felt like an eternity ("Not even close," Zeke informed them when Martin complained along those lines), the unlikely threesome found themselves standing in the queue for Window Nine. Martin and Zelda stepped forward and handed in their latest round of pointless paperwork while Zeke hung back.

The girl behind the desk took their forms without looking up and flipped through them quickly. She nodded her pretty blonde head. "OK," she said. "We just need to get your ID cards printed, then you can go on to the next floor. Step over to the white background there and we'll snap a quick photo." She finally looked up at them, her gaze traveling past Martin and Zelda. "Oh, hey, Ezekiel!" she said sweetly as she stood up and moved toward a camera mounted on a tripod near her desk. Her high heels made little click-clicking sounds as she walked. She smiled over her shoulder as she bent forward to turn on her camera, showing off the perfect roundness of her ass.

"Hey, Lila," Zeke said, pulling at his tie again.

Lila gestured for Zelda to step in front of the lens with a wave of her prettily manicured hand. Red-faced and seething, Zelda went and stood in front of the white passport-photo-style background.

"Oh, get a load of this one, Ezekiel," the beautiful Lila said with an ugly little laugh as she peered at Zelda through the lens of her camera. "A crown and everything. And what a bitchy look on her face! Who is she supposed to be, huh? The Princess of Cuntistan?"

A deep, guttural, inhuman sound came out of Zelda then, and she launched herself at Lila just as the camera's flash went off. As the two tussled on the floor, Lila seemed to be making a concerted effort to pull Zelda's corset top clear off. Zelda's frantic clawing and flailing had Lila's mini skirt riding up her thighs. Martin found himself conflicted as to which girl he should root for.

Unlike Martin, Zeke did not stand idly by and watch the cat fight. He dove into the fray. Which of his lovers Zeke was trying to spare wasn't immediately clear, but Martin would have been hard-pressed to say he didn't enjoy the sight of both girls raining blows meant for each other down on Zeke Zabar's wild-haired head.

The whole scuffle probably lasted less than a minute. Just as two uniformed security officers started jogging toward the scene, Zeke dragged Zelda to her feet and pulled her away from Lila, who struggled to sit up and straighten her blouse. "You filthy fucking whore!" Zelda shrieked, bucking in Zeke's arms. Droplets of perspiration flew off her as she raged. "Disease-ridden slut!"

"Alright, that's enough," Zeke said. One of his eyes was starting to swell and blood dribbled from a scratch across his cheek.

"What the fuck?" Lila shouted, getting to her feet.

"This one's a hard case," Zeke told her while Zelda struggled to break free of his grasp. He leaned toward Lila a little bit. "Mental problems," he told her. "Big time."

"You're telling me," Lila said. She reached out to touch Zeke's cheek. "Are you OK?"

Zelda growled.

Zeke tightened his grip on her and pulled her further away from Lila. "I'm alright," he said. "You?"

"I'm OK," Lila said. She smiled and stepped closer to Zeke again. "Maybe we can lick each other's wounds later," she said seductively.

Zelda became a wild animal in a corset and the security guards stepped in to keep her from pouncing on Lila again.

Lila shook her head at Zeke, who shrugged back at her helplessly. She smoothed her skirt and stepped behind her camera once more. "You," she said to Martin. "Stand over there and say, 'Cheese.'"

Martin did as he was told. "Ch—," he said as the flash went off in his face. He stood there blinking a minute, vaguely aware of Zeke talking to Zelda in hushed tones next to him.

"Here you go," Lila said, taking two plastic ID cards from a machine and pressing them into Martin's hand. "Get them out of here, will you?" she said to the security guards.

"You know," Zeke said, giving Zelda a very meaningful look. "I think I can take it from here. Really, guys. This one's a live wire. Groups of people seem to freak her out. It's probably safer if I just get her downstairs on my own."

The guards furrowed their brows. "You sure?" One of them said, his hand on some kind of nightstick at his belt. "Maybe we should expedite her."

"Nah," Zeke said. "They've been swamped over at the expediting office. Really. I've got this. We're not going to have any more problems here, are we, miss?" He looked beseechingly at Zelda.

"Right," Zelda said, ceasing her struggle and shrugging out of Zeke's grasp. "Sir." Her cheeks were flushed and her eyes were bright, but she seemed to be in control of herself. She patted her sweat-damp hair and smoothed her skirt.

"See?" Zeke said brightly to the two guards. "It was just a misunderstanding, I think."

"OK," the guard with the nightstick said. He looked a little bit relieved.

"You holler if you need us, though," the other one chimed in.

"Will do, guys," Zeke said, reaching out to shake their hands. "And thanks. Thanks very much for helping out."

"No problem," one of them said. The other one just nodded.

"Let's go," Zeke said as the guards turned and started walking away. One of them looked back over his shoulder, and Zeke hustled Martin and Zelda forward, hurrying toward a gray door at the end of the room. "Got your IDs?" he asked.

Martin held his up and passed the other one to Zelda. He glanced at his own and sighed. Lila had caught him on the "ch" part of "cheese." His lips were all puckered up like a fish's and his eyes were half-closed. His usually neat brown hair looked matted and damp and his cheeks were flushed. This could end up being his photo ID for all eternity? Was Hell ever going to stop sucking?

"Hey," Zelda said, looking at her own ID card. "That bitch!" The photo showed a red-faced Zelda lunging toward the camera, mouth open in a primal scream. She looked back at Lila over her shoulder, doing a close approximation of the demonic-smoldering-coal thing with her eyes.

Lila was looking back at her and laughing. "No retakes," she called out in a sing-songy voice. "Welcome to Hell, bitch!"

Zelda lunged like she was going to go after Lila again, but Zeke grabbed her by the arm, commandeered her ID card, swiped it through a card reader next to the door, and shoved her through. Martin followed. Zeke let the metal door bang shut behind them and slumped against it, his breathing uneven.

"It's like you're trying to make me send you downstairs, you know that?" he said to Zelda. He touched his swollen eye, then his cheek, looked at Zelda reproachfully, then took off down the hallway. "Come on," he said. "Follow me."

Zeke led Martin and Zelda along a narrow, empty corridor with low ceilings. They were in an older part of the intake office now. Martin could tell because the hallway was paved with chipped, scuffed black floor tiles and the walls were painted a dark and dingy gray. Martin paused in front of a mural. It looked for all the world like *Saturn Devouring His Son*.

"Goya?" he asked Zeke, impressed in spite of himself.

Zelda stood back and made a big point of not looking at either one of them. She was strangely quiet. Martin wasn't sure whether she'd been hurt in her brawl with Lila, but he suspected her pride, at least, had taken a serious hit.

"Yeah." Zeke nodded, looking at the grotesque mural Martin was eyeing. "Goya."

"Did he paint this himself?"

"Legend has it that he required some…persuasion… from the demons. But, yeah. It's supposed to be entirely his own work."

"Goya's down here, too, then?" Martin was oddly relieved to find that, as a damned soul, he was turning out to be in some very good company.

"Pretty much every great artist, writer, and musician in the history of the world is down here somewhere," Zeke said.

"How come?" Martin was stunned.

"You name it," Zeke said. "Lots of those tortured, creative types get brought in for drunkenness, pride, lust, envy, that kind of thing. The ones who make it big, who find commercial success, go down for avarice, of course. Wastefulness. Wantonness."

"Wow," Martin said. "What about, like, the Renaissance greats? Artists whose work glorified God?"

"What about them?" Zeke answered.

"Are they all down here, too? Like Michelangelo. He sculpted the Pietà, for crying out loud. Are you telling me he's burning in Hell right this minute?"

"I guess you didn't come through the main lobby," Zeke said. "Or you would have seen some of his work. Big pair of demons made of black marble. They're huge. Two, three times the size of a man. You can't miss them. Beautiful things. In a scare-the-shit-out-of-you kind of way."

"I can't believe this," Martin said. "All of them? Raphael? Bellini? Titian?"

Zeke waved a hand dismissively. "Idolaters, all of them."

"Nerds!" Zelda fake-coughed into her hand.

"One nerd," Zeke corrected her, pointing at Martin. "And one victim." He pointed to himself. "It's not my fault I've had fifty-nine lifetimes of culture crammed down my throat...not to mention the innumerable modern Intro to Art History classes I've had to sit through! Van AssMan studies all this shit for fun."

Martin sighed. Oh, the academic bowl questions he could have answered back on Earth if only he'd been afforded fifty-nine lifetimes in which to study.

"So," Martin said to Zeke, turning his thoughts back to the artists he'd always admired and their alleged idolatry. "Do you mean to tell me that God damned some of history's greatest painters and sculptors to Hell because they dared to celebrate Him with their God-given artistic talents?"

"Eh," Zeke said. "I don't think it works that way."

"Well, how does it work, then?"

"Who freaking cares?" Zelda exploded. "Can we just get going?" She was breathing a little heavily with pent-up anger. Her recent fistfight had loosened her corset and a little more flesh than usual was spilling out over the top. Martin did his best to look her in the eye.

"I'm sorry, Zelda" he said. "I didn't realize you were in a huge screaming hurry to burn. Sorry if I happen to take an interest in my surroundings. Sorry if I care about fine art and the people who make it. A good number of whom, I might add, were artists who lived during the freaking Renaissance, a time period you supposedly love enough to recreate with your fellow corset-wearing freaks at festivals." Zelda looked down at her medieval-slipper-clad feet, embarrassed, but Martin was on a roll. "And excuuuuse me," he shouted. "For trying to figure out how the system that determines how we're going to spend the rest of eternity works!"

"Let's everybody just calm down," Zeke said. "And keep moving." He looked up and down the hallway a little nervously.

It hadn't escaped Martin's attention that the corridor they were in was spiraling gently downward. He wasn't especially anxious to see where it led. The grisly images from Demon TV were still fresh in his mind.

"I haven't done an intake for anybody specifically damned by the man upstairs," Zeke said, finally answering Martin's question about God as they all set off again. "I mean, we've all sinned, right? There probably isn't a Permanent Record on file anywhere in the afterlife that's completely blemish-free. But I don't think God uses those black marks as reasons to punish people. It's more like the boss down here looks for any excuse he can find to claim as many souls as possible. Like the two of you. You weren't sent here by any kind of divine order; you messed up a little bit and got brought in by demons looking for easy marks. Me, too, for that matter. I don't think anybody has to damn a soul for it to get stuck here. I think most people end up inadvertently damning themselves. The thing about staying out of Hell is, from what I understand, you have to at least try."

"We tried!" Zelda snapped. "And now look at us."

"You followed a demon through a mall," Zeke said.

"We were being chased!" Zelda protested.

"Yeah," Zeke said. "And you saw what you thought was an easy way out of the situation and you took it, didn't you?"

Zelda only huffed in reply.

Martin stopped walking again to ponder another mural. It kind of looked like the *Mona Lisa*, except the top of her head was exploding, red flames shooting in all directions, and tiny demons were clawing their ways out of her mouth and eye sockets. In the background, tortured souls writhed in agony across the famously bleak landscape. "Is this...? It can't be."

Zeke laughed. "It is," he said. "DaVinci. I've been told he was supposed to paint an exact reproduction, but tried to rebel a little bit. The boss liked this version so much, of course, he left it up, but I understand poor Leonardo is still rotting in a solitary cell for his insolence."

"Holy shit," Martin breathed.

Zeke kept walking and gestured for Martin and Zelda to follow. "It doesn't matter anyway," Zeke said. "They're going to renovate this part of the office next. Going with a red motif throughout the building, I hear. They'll paper over all of this, I bet."

Martin looked the bizarre rendition of the *Mona Lisa* up and down again and sighed. "I guess we're lucky we got to see it when we did, then," he said.

"Yeah," Zelda said. "It's our lucky fucking day."

Chapter 15

As they neared the end of the downward-spiraling passageway, the dull gray paint broken up by masterfully rendered murals gave way to rough-hewn stone walls. The ceiling and floor, too, were soon made entirely of dull gray stone. What appeared to be torches lined the walls, replacing the more modern fluorescent lighting of the previous corridor. Upon closer inspection, Martin could see that the torches were just replicas, wall sconces with flickering bulbs and stained-glass shades shaped to resemble orange and red flames. He admired the decorator's attention to detail as well as his pragmatism.

As they made their way carefully over the uneven stone, Martin heard the distinct sound of rushing water ahead of them.

"What's that?" Zelda asked, stopping in her tracks.

"It's a river," Zeke said. "Come on. We have to get across. Once we're on the other side, I can try to get you out of here."

Zeke kept walking and Martin followed close behind him. Zelda hung back a little, looking around at the stone corridor with trepidation. The sound of the water got louder and louder. Soon, the tight passageway opened onto an expansive cavern.

"Whoa," Martin breathed. The floor was shiny, wet obsidian. Stalactites hung down from the ceiling in a menacing, but breathtakingly beautiful, array. The slick floor sloped down to a vast river of rushing black water. A burst of cool air was a welcome relief from the heat of the intake office's overachieving furnaces.

Martin craned his neck, but he couldn't see the other side. "Wait," he said. "This can't possibly be...?"

Zeke laughed. "Next stop on the tour," he said with a grand arm gesture. "The River Styx! No flash photography, please."

"Holy shit!" Martin said, laughing in disbelief. "It's real!"

"It's huge," Zeke said. "It somehow manages to wend its way through almost all of our regional intake offices."

"Almost all of them?" Martin said, still staring, transfixed, at the mythical waters.

"It misses a few remote branches," Zeke said. "But they've almost all built replicas now. You know. River envy or whatever. But this one here's the real deal." Zeke actually seemed a little bit proud of his new workplace.

Everything about Hell was supremely annoying and eternal agony might just await him at the end of his journey downstairs, but Martin had to admit that he was fascinated by all the wonders he'd beheld since his arrival.

"I can't believe it," Martin kept gushing. "The myths were true! But this river is ancient, older than ancient." Martin furrowed his brow. The river's presence suddenly didn't seem to mesh with the newly renovated upstairs portion of the intake office. "Why haven't they just, I dunno, paved over it or built a bridge here or something by now?"

"I asked the same question at orientation," Zeke said.

"There was an orientation?" Martin found himself wanting to know everything about Hell and its inner workings.

"Of course," Zeke said. "You think this red blazer was magically imbued with everything I needed to know to escort the damned through the heinously long intake process and help them reach their final destinations?" He rolled his eyes. "This is my job, Van AssMan. I take it seriously."

"OK," Martin said. "Sorry." He didn't want to piss off his only source of insider info, his own personal talking travelogue of Hell. Not to mention his only hope of escape. "What did they say about the bridge?"

"Well," Zeke said, leading them down to the water's edge. "I said I thought it seemed inefficient to have to take every soul across one at a time, you know? 'Time is money, right?' I said. 'Even down here.' I suggested a bridge or some kind of an overhead gondola ride."

"A gondola would be nice," Martin said. "Scenic. And pleasantly unexpected."

"Right?" Zeke said. "Only they shot me down. They said the boss likes the effect a good old-fashioned river crossing has on the damned. Shakes them up a bit. Humbles them. After I'd been here a little while, I could totally see his point."

Martin nodded. He saw the point, too. All that black water swirling between him and the unseen horrors waiting on the opposite bank was definitely daunting.

Just then, a raft loomed out of the shadows. It cut through the choppy water without a sound, its eerily silent arrival unnerving at best. A skeleton wearing a black hooded cloak and a ghastly grin manned the tiller.

"Charon?" Martin whispered to Zeke as he stepped aboard.

"Nah," Zeke said with a little chuckle, settling himself on the raft like a pro. He sat cross-legged near the front.

Martin wobbled a bit as he boarded, fighting to keep his balance.

"Charon retired eons ago." Zeke grabbed one of the skeleton's arms and flapped it at Martin, who almost fell over backwards as the bony hand danced in front of his face. "It's just plastic," Zeke said, laughing. "The whole thing's pretty much for show nowadays." He shifted his weight around to rock the raft back and forth in the water, much to Martin's consternation. "See?" he said when they didn't tip over. "The raft is on a track and everything."

"Like at Disney World," Martin said. "The 'It's a Small World' ride."

"I've never been to the Magic Kingdom. Or any kind of an amusement park at all for that matter," Zeke said, not wholly unbitter. "Can you believe that shit? Not even once in fifty-nine lifetimes."

"Sorry," Martin mumbled and he sat down a little clumsily next to Zeke. He suddenly felt ashamed of having been taken to Disney World three different times by his doting, éclair-eating parents. Martin had especially loved spending time at Epcot. Each time they went, his parents had shown endless patience with him while he spent hours exploring the interactive exhibits there. His dad was always as enthralled as he was, his mom always smiling at both of them, taking their pictures, and buying souvenirs. Then, they'd all made a point of enjoying horizon-expanding foreign food at one World Showcase eatery or another and, of course, indulged in French pastries for dessert.

Martin blinked. He thought some water from the Styx must have splashed into his eyes.

"Hey, Zel," Zeke called. Zelda was still standing on the obsidian riverbank, her eyes wide, her face pale. "Let's go."

"I'm not coming," Zelda said, backing up. She slipped a little on the wet rock, regained her balance, and turned away from the rushing river and started heading back to the stone passageway.

"Babe!" Zeke called. He stood up and stepped off the raft, setting Martin to bobbing up and down so he had to grab the plastic skeleton for balance. "You have to come. There's no other way to get where we need to go."

"No way," she said.

Zeke caught up to her and grabbed her by the shoulders.

"Zelda," he said. "Stop being difficult. We need to go. Now. Before anyone else comes along. You're not the only two facing damnation right now, OK? Another escort could be along any minute with his charge."

"I can't," Zelda said. She started to cry a little, her lip trembling pitifully. "Zeke, please. I can't. I'll take whatever punishment they give me, but I can't go out on the water. Not like this. Not subject to gravity. I'll sink."

"Babe," Zeke said, running a hand through his hair. "I don't understand."

"I drowned, Zeke!" Zelda said. "And so did you! How can you not remember this?"

"Aw, Zel. I do remember." He stroked her arm gently. "I do. But this isn't the same thing. It's perfectly safe, I swear. Sometimes I cross and come back five, six times a shift."

Zelda shook her head and turned away.

"Besides," Zeke tried. "You're already dead! I mean, even if we fell in—which we won't!—what's the worst that could happen?"

"Actually," Martin chimed in. "I think the water's supposed to give you immortality or protection, something like that. Right? It might be awesome to fall in. Remember Achilles?"

"That's just a myth, asshole," Zeke snapped at him. "Don't help." He looked back at Zelda. "Nobody's falling in, babe. I promise."

"I'm not going," Zelda said. "That's my final word."

"OK." Zeke sighed, putting his hands up in surrender. "Alright. You don't have to come." He reached into his pocket, took out a shiny box, tapped something into his hand, and held it out to Zelda. "But you do, for your own good, have to chew this."

Zelda looked at the thing in Zeke's palm with disdain. "What is it?" she asked. "It looks like a breath mint."

"It is," Zeke said. "You reek. Really foul. Must be lake breath or something."

Zelda reddened and popped the proffered tablet into her mouth.

Zeke waited next to her on the bank, counting quietly to himself. When he reached thirty, he looked up at Zelda and smiled. "Shall we, m'lady?" he asked, holding out his elbow like he was offering to escort her to prom.

Zelda swayed on the spot, then stumbled toward Zeke, giggling, and he caught her. "Atta girl," he muttered.

"Come on." He dragged her aboard the raft while she laughed hysterically in his arms.

"Did you just roofie her?!" Martin asked, appalled. "Did you just roofie your ex-girlfriend? That's diabolical! Even for a tour guide in Hell!"

"Relax, Fartin," Zeke said, shifting some of Zelda's weight off him as they both settled onto the raft. "She's fine."

"No!" Martin said, waving an accusatory finger at Zeke. "I won't relax. You can't do that to her! I'm going to report you! I'm going to—"

"You're going to shut the fuck up," Zeke said. His black eye and scratched cheek made him look pretty tough. Martin backed down. "It wasn't a roofie, OK? It was a high-grade, fiendishly strong mood-altering pharmaceutical designed by Hell's top research scientists. They give them to escorts to use on difficult cases, souls who freak out about heading downstairs or whatever. It's not always in our own best interests to use physical force." Zeke pointed to his swollen eye. "It's standard operating procedure, Van AssMan. She'll be perfectly fine."

"So, you've done this before?"

Zelda was laughing and looking up the robe of the plastic skeleton. "Peek-a-boo!" she called. "Guys! Look! He's got a boner! Get it? A boner? 'Cause he's a skeleton? 'Cause he's made of bones?"

"No," Zeke said, pulling Zelda out from under the tillerman's robes and putting an arm around her. "I haven't, technically, done this before. Zelda's my first."

"Aw," she said. "And you're mine, babe. Woo hoo!" She laughed and splashed a hand in the water. "You're my first, but not my last, babe! FYI, I'm gonna bang Marty here before this is all over to get back at you for that photo-booth bitch. 'K? He died without ever getting laid, which is pretty sad."

Martin blushed and stared down at the raft.

Zelda splashed some of the river water at Zeke. "Woo hoo!" she shouted again. "Let's rock and roll! Get this pleasure cruise started!"

"OK," Zeke said. "This is a little awkward. But, you have to pay."

"Buy my ticket for me, babe?" Zelda asked, wrapping her wet arms around Zeke's neck. "I'm dead and I don't have my wallet."

"Pay!" Martin said happily, his eyes brightening. "Of course! Yes! A coin!" He started patting his pockets. "I've got to have some change on me. Hang on."

"Your money's no good here," Zeke said.

"But in the myth, it's a coin, a coin left in the deceased's mouth, I think, that's used to pay Charon for his services." Martin looked absolutely crestfallen.

"Those stories are really old," Zeke said. "Back then, there were only, like, a handful of currencies in use. Now, forget about it. Fluctuating exchange rates, the freaking Euro. How much math do you want this plastic skeleton to do?"

Martin sighed.

"You have to pay a different way now," Zeke said. "You have to offer up something that's really important to you. Yell out your sacrifice or toss something valuable into the river."

"I know! I've got it!" Zelda sat up on her knees, bright-eyed and smiling. She ripped the gold circlet off her head and chucked it into the water. It landed with a splash and sank unnaturally slowly below the dark surface. "Ooooh!" Zelda said, watching it go. "Sunken treasure!" She laughed.

"OK," Zeke said. "Now you." He nodded to Martin.

Martin looked perplexed. He patted his empty pants pockets again. "I don't have anything," he said. "I don't have anything to throw in."

"Nothing?" Zeke said. "Nothing at all?"

Martin shrugged helplessly. "Sometimes I'm fond of Zelda," he admitted. "But I can't see throwing her overboard. It would kind of defeat the purpose of trying to save her."

Zelda crawled over to Martin on the raft. "That's so sweet," she said. "Sometimes I'm fond of you, too." She pursed her lips in his direction and made a loud, wet smacking noise.

"On second thought..." Martin said.

"Take off your pants." Zeke pulled Zelda back over to sit next to him.

"Excuse me?"

"Take off your pants," Zeke repeated.

"What for?" Martin asked.

"Trust me," Zeke said. "Mr. Bones will let you cross in your skivvies."

Martin started doing as he was told, standing up and turning away from Zeke and Zelda as he unzipped his fly and shimmied out of his khakis. One of his sneakers got stuck in his pants leg and he had to hop up and down on the bobbing raft to free his foot.

"Take it off, Martin!" Zelda screamed. "Take it aaaaallll off! Wooooooooooo!" She put her fingers in her mouth and whistled like a construction worker.

Martin was extremely embarrassed by his scrawny legs and felt much nakeder than he really was as he held his pants out over the river.

"Drop 'em in," Zeke said.

Martin hesitated.

"Do it!"

Martin let his pants fall, watched them vanish into the River Styx. The raft started with a jerk and Martin almost fell over. "I don't get it," he admitted as he sat back down a little clumsily.

Zelda started singing "It's a Small World" as loudly as she could.

"It wasn't really about your pants," Zeke said. "You had to give up some of your pride to get across the river."

"Oh," Martin said. For some reason, that embarrassed him even more than riding an underworld ferry in his boxer shorts. "What about you?" he said. "You didn't have to give anything up?"

"I've already paid," Zeke said darkly. "I've got unlimited rides for the foreseeable part of eternity."

"What did you throw into the river?" Martin asked.

Zelda trailed a hand along in the water. "Hey!" She said. "Should we skinny dip?" She jumped to her feet and started trying to work her medieval costume up over her head.

"Sit down," Zeke said, annoyed, pulling her voluminous skirts back into place. "Sit down and stay quiet, OK?"

"Humph," Zelda said. "I remember when you used to be fun, Zeke Zabar." She flapped his necktie up and down. "Now look at you. You're about as much fun as this guy over here." She jerked her thumb at the skeleton steering their boat. "Hey," she said to the skeleton. "Do you want to swim naked with me?" She pulled at the top of her corset.

Zeke stopped her and pulled her dress back up. Martin was just a tad disappointed. He shifted around on the raft so the crotch of his underwear didn't show. "How long is this drug going to last?" he asked.

"That's a fair question," Zeke said. "I'm really not sure."

Zelda was on her feet again, dancing with the skeleton.

Zeke sighed and ran his hand through his hair.

Martin looked ahead, trying to see the opposite riverbank. A spooky mist obscured any view he might have had. Martin shivered. He was cold sitting there on the water in his underwear. Crossing the River Styx was definitely starting to lose some of its appeal.

"Alright. That's enough," Zeke said. He stood up and started tugging on Zelda again, who'd been kissing the plastic tillerman with relish.

"He kisses like you, Van AssMan," she said, laughing, as Zeke settled her back down onto the raft. Then, she looked around, suddenly very serious. "Hey," she said. "Are we there yet?"

"Almost, babe," Zeke told her, sounding tired. "Almost."

Zelda smiled and started humming "It's a Small World" quietly to herself. "When I was little," she said to no one in particular. "My parents took us to Disney World and Jenny cried on the spinning teacup ride. That was before we hated each other. I remember holding her hand." Zelda hummed a sadder "Small World" tune now.

"Hey babe?" she said to Zeke.

"Yeah?" Zeke answered.

"In our next life, I'm going to take you to the Magic Kingdom. We're gonna ride the tea cups and the Small World boats, OK?"

"OK," Zeke said with a sad little smile. "Sounds fun."

"Yeah," Zelda said. "It will be. You'd look awesome in mouse ears." She started humming happily again.

The raft started slowing down. Some of the mist was parting and Martin could see the shore. "I think we're there," he said.

"Yeah," Zeke said. "Hang on. There's a little jolt at the end here."

The raft glided silently up to the obsidian bank, then lodged itself there with a gentle bump.

"Ahhhh!" Zelda tumbled into the water without even trying to save herself.

"Damn it," Zeke said.

Zelda struggled to stand up in waist-high black water. "Babe?" she said, sounding calm, but confused. "I think I'm drowning again. Am I drowning?"

"You're not," Zeke assured her. "Martin, help me."

Together, they dragged a soaking-wet Zelda up onto the riverbank where she lay like a washed-ashore rag doll.

The raft with its plastic ferryman turned and headed back the way they'd come.

"Shit," Zeke said. "He's going back already. That means there must be someone else waiting to cross."

"Guys?" Zelda said, still lying on her back. "I'm wet. And I can't feel my face." She made fish lips and scrunched up her eyebrows.

"We have to get out of here," Zeke said. "Zelda, can you walk?"

"I think so," she said, not making any effort to move from where she lay on the riverbank. She screwed her eyes shut tight. "Am I doing it?" she asked.

"Yeah, babe," Zeke lied. "Great job."

Zelda flashed him a wide smile.

"How far do we have to go?" Martin asked. "You said we could get out from this side of the river. Tell me there's a fire exit around here somewhere."

"A fire exit? In Hell?"

"Right," Martin said. "Eternal flames. Fire and brimstone. Never mind."

"Get her feet," Zeke said, putting his arms under Zelda's shoulders.

Martin grabbed Zelda around the knees. Her wet costume was soaking his boxer shorts through, making him fairly miserable and even more embarrassed than he had been when his underwear was dry. He wondered suddenly if Zeke had been fucking with him back when they boarded the raft, if maybe it hadn't been entirely necessary to pants himself to get across the river. After all, Zeke enjoyed unlimited rides with all his clothes on.

"This way," Zeke said, moving away from the water's edge and pulling Zelda's dead weight with him. Martin stumbled along behind him, struggling with his half of Zelda's body.

At the entrance to what appeared to be a stone tunnel at the back of the cavern, Martin slipped on the wet rock and fell hard, dragging Zeke and Zelda down with him. He landed clumsily on top of Zelda and sliced his knee open on the sharp obsidian. Zelda moaned and opened her eyes, staring right at Martin as if she were seeing him for the first time.

"Zeke," she said. "I love you."

"That's Martin," Zeke said, getting to his feet and smoothing his damp pants and blazer.

"Oh," Zelda said, tilting her head all the way backwards to look at Zeke upside-down. "I love you, too, Martin," she told him.

Zeke looked seriously stressed. "We have to get through this tunnel," he said. "But it's close quarters. And it's steep. I don't know how we're going to carry her."

"I don't want to tell you how to do your job," Martin said, standing up and pulling his damp sweatshirt as far down over his underwear as it would go. "But why don't we just take that escalator over there?" Just to the right of the narrow tunnel entrance, a wide escalator hummed efficiently. Martin swore he heard mall-style muzak playing, even. The whole thing was suddenly very inviting in spite of his usual aversion to shopping malls and their dastardly accoutrements.

"That leads to the next round of windows and paperwork," Zeke said. "I'm trying to circumvent all that." He ran his hand through his crazy hair and sighed. "Unless you wanted to fill out some more forms before you go?"

"No," Martin said. "Absolutely not." Even the nerd had had enough of question answering for one eternity. "The tunnel it is." He swiped at his bloody knee and sighed. He knew he hadn't seen the half of it yet, but Hell was definitely taking a toll on him.

Zeke bent over Zelda, who appeared to be passed out. "Help me lift her," Zeke said. "I'll try a fireman's carry."

They hoisted Zelda up onto Zeke's shoulder. He was tall, and Zelda looked strange folded in half so high above the ground.

"Her face is in your ass," Martin observed.

"I'm aware," Zeke said. He shifted her around a little bit, trying to get comfortable. Her big, wet skirts were dripping all over him, soaking his red blazer and tie. "Let's go," Zeke said. "Before that raft comes back."

There was an awful sound then as Zelda threw up all over the back of Zeke's work pants and the ancient obsidian bank of the River Styx.

"Oh," Martin said. "That's too bad."

"Fuck my afterlife," Zeke said with a sigh of resignation. "Let's just go."

Chapter 16

The rocky tunnel was, as Zeke had warned, narrow and upward-sloping. Zeke trudged along in front, carrying Zelda, and Martin tried to keep up, his injured knee smarting with every step. He felt absolutely ridiculous climbing up the stone incline in his underwear.

How did I get here? he kept asking himself. *How did I go from being just another nerd at an international film festival to a lost soul trying to escape Satan's clutches, scrambling through the depths of Hell in my underwear with the likes of Zeke Zabar and Zelda Kozikowski?*

Zeke stopped a minute to shift his burden around and Martin almost ran right into him. After just the briefest of pauses, they started moving again. Zeke seemed surprisingly strong and determined as he bore Zelda uphill. Martin reluctantly admired him in a way he hadn't before.

"Thanks for helping us by the way," Martin said, a little out of breath.

"No sweat," Zeke said. "It's just a little farther, OK? Then we'll take a break."

"So, what's this big plan you've got cooked up?" Martin tried not to sound at all skeptical.

"Well," Zeke said. "I made a few calls to the Soul Reassignment Office. They're aware of your defection, obviously." He looked over his shoulder at Martin. "Apparently you gave two of their Seekers the slip at a shopping mall."

"Yeah," Martin said. "I figured. We didn't know those guys were from Soul Reassignment at the time, obviously, or we probably would have opted to go with them over the demon."

"Are you sure?" Zeke asked, smiling over his shoulder. "Zelda seemed quite taken with…what was his name? Dmitri?" He might have sounded a tad bitter.

"Well," Martin said. "You know Zelda."

"Yes," Zeke said a little coldly. "I do."

They walked a little further without speaking. The only sounds Martin heard were their footfalls on the stone floor of the tunnel and the shifting of Zelda's inert body over Zeke's shoulder. She moaned softly once, then was quiet again.

"So, you called the office?" Martin prompted. He still wanted to hear the rest of Zeke's big escape plan. "What did they say?"

"Yeah," Zeke said. "I called them. They're not too pleased with you, you know. With any of us, actually. Our little escape act caused everyone over there quite a bit of trouble. I think a few people lost their jobs. They've had to step up security, change some of their intake procedures. Don't be expecting a hero's welcome or anything when you get back."

"OK," Martin said. He really hated it when people didn't like him. He almost thought he'd rather stay in Hell where nobody held a specific grudge against him than go back to the Soul Reassignment Office where he knew everyone was annoyed with him, where everyone probably knew that he now had a black mark on his Permanent

Record. But, then again, he still hadn't forgotten what they had seen on the waiting-room television screen.

"Anyway," Zeke went on. "They've agreed to send a couple folks to meet you guys when you get back to Earth. Just go with them this time, Fartin, OK? Trust me. Because if it gets out that you escaped from Hell—and I'm pretty sure it will get out—you can bet your damned, boxer-shorted ass that there'll be plenty of demons on the way, hell-bent on bringing you back. And there won't be an intake process the second time around, Van AssMan. They'll just send you straight down to the pits. Capiche?"

"Go with the suits," Martin said. "Got it. No problem. But, can I ask how we're supposed to get back to Earth in the first place?"

"You can."

Martin waited. Then, "Right," he said. "OK. How are we supposed to get back to Earth in the first place?"

"I thought you'd never ask," Zeke said, smiling infuriatingly at Martin over the top of Zelda's rear end. "You're going to fly. Hitch a ride, actually. That is…" Zeke frowned. "If you can. I don't honestly know for sure. We're just going to have to go with the flow." Zeke shifted Zelda's weight around again and she sighed. Martin felt a little sorry for her. She was going to have a definite head rush from being upside-down for so long. "We're here," Zeke said. "Let's wait right here."

The tunnel had opened up onto a small cavern. The walls glowed an eerie red. Stalactites and stalagmites looked like monstrous teeth ready to chomp down on anything that came between them. Martin didn't want to seem like a Negative Nelly, but he really didn't see how being stuck in a creepy cavern was getting them any closer to Earth and their rescuers from the Soul Reassignment Office.

Zeke stepped to the side and knelt down. With a sigh of relief, he deposited Zelda in a heap on the cavern floor where she stirred and then was still. Zeke rubbed his shoulder and cracked his neck a little. "She's heavier than she looks," he said. "A real ton of bricks."

Martin sat down on the other side of Zelda. He brushed some damp hair away from her forehead. "I hope she's going to be OK," he said. She looked pale, most of her makeup long gone; even her lips were almost white.

"She will be," Zeke said, but he didn't sound as confident as Martin would have liked. "Listen, Van Assen." Martin looked up at the use of his real name. "Make sure she's alright up there, will you? Look after her until you get back to the Soul Reassignment Office?"

"I got her this far, didn't I?" Martin said.

"Yeah," Zeke said. "I guess you did." He was quiet a minute. "How was it on Earth? Visiting people and whatnot."

"It was…pretty awful," Martin said. "Sad. Depressing. Entirely pointless. My mother's up there right now serving éclairs to her dinner guests. Éclairs! Can you believe that shit?"

"And my mom…?"

"She's OK," Martin said. "I really think she is. We might have freaked her out a little bit…" Zeke looked up sharply. "On accident, of course! Totally on accident. Who knew she was a real psychic? Right? But she's doing OK. Her clairvoyant business seems to be going well at least.

And she has your brother." Martin didn't think Zeke needed to know that Jude had been a total asshole and seemed to have taken over Zeke's room, of course, but maybe he could guess.

Zeke snorted. "My brother," he said. "Poor Ma. She did her best for us, you know? I know what my family must have looked like to you, Van Assen, but I've had way worse. She had a hard life, my mom. I really think she did her best for us."

Martin didn't know what to say. "Well," he tried. "Maybe you can look in on her sometime, you know? Help her out somehow in your next life? Do you ever do that? Go back and visit people you've known in one of your previous lifetimes?"

"No," Zeke said. "I usually try not to. And, Martin, listen. I'm not going back for another lifetime."

"What?" Martin said.

"I'm not going with you. I'm not going back to Earth."

"Why not?" Martin asked.

Zeke shrugged. "Lots of reasons," he said. "For one thing, I hate it there."

"Zeke," Martin said. "Look around! You're in Hell! Do you honestly prefer it here?"

"Kind of," Zeke said with a shrug. "Yeah, I kind of do. I don't have any sort of purpose to fulfill down here, for one thing. I just slog back and forth across the Styx, shuffle people along through paperwork queues. That's it. I'll never have to start over again. I get to be…this," he gestured to his rumpled, wet, ruined jacket and tie. "Right here. Forever."

Martin shook his head. "You have to spend your days with the dregs of society," Martin said. "Monsters. Abominations."

"Most of my intakes aren't that bad," Zeke said. "Sure, there's the occasional dirtbag, scum-of-the-Earth type, but most of our clientele is just like you." A smile crept across his face. "Actually," he said. "Most of my intakes are a lot less trouble than you've been so far, Fartin Van AssMan."

"I just can't believe you're choosing this," Martin said. He didn't know why he was getting so worked up over the fate of freaking Zeke Zabar, but he was. If he'd been wearing pants, he would have stood up and started pacing in frustration. "I can't believe you're choosing to stay behind in Hell when there might be another option—any other option!"

"I don't expect you to understand," Zeke said. "Just promise me you'll take care of Zelda."

"Take care of her yourself!" Martin said. "Come back with us. Get a new assignment. Help her through her whole next life if you care about her so much!"

"Even if I wanted to," Zeke said. "Which, like I said, I don't. I can't."

"Whatever." Martin stroked Zelda's hair again, made sure she was still breathing. She sighed a little and pulled her knees up to her chest.

"I signed a contract here," Zeke said. "Five hundred Earth years before my soul is potentially up for grabs again."

"Holy shit!" Martin said. "Five hundred years!"

Zeke waved a hand dismissively. "That's nothing, really," he said. "Especially compared to the eternal damnation I was facing otherwise. You just don't seem to get how unimportant time is in the grand scheme of things. You've probably been down here for several Earth months already, and I bet you didn't even realize it."

"What?" Martin said. "I have? Wow. My afterlife is really flying by."

"There's another thing, too," Zeke said. "And I'm only telling you this so you can explain it to Zelda later. If I did ever go back someday—and, trust me, I won't—I wouldn't be able to remember any of it."

"Any of what?" Martin asked. "Your time in Hell?"

"That," Zeke said. "And also the fifty-nine lives I've lived, including the last one where I met this freaky-but-awesome Renaissance-faire-loving gamer chick named Zelda Kozikowski." Zeke smiled ruefully. "Remember you asked me what I gave to Charon? What meaningful thing I had to sacrifice to cross the Styx for the first time?"

"You gave up your Earthly memories?"

"Yeah," Zeke said. "At least, I gave up my unusual ability to retain them from human lifetime to human lifetime. The memories were all I had that meant anything to me," Zeke said. "And, probably, I'm better off without all of them, anyway. A few were really nice, I guess, but most of them were complete shit."

"So, you won't remember Zelda," Martin said.

"Not if I go back to Earth, no," Zeke said. He sat with his elbows on his knees and clasped his hands. He leaned his head back against the cavern wall and closed his eyes.

"And you're determined not to go back," Martin said.

"Extremely," Zeke confirmed.

"So you'll never fulfill your purpose," Martin said.

"I guess not," Zeke replied with a shrug. "I gave it a fair shot, though, didn't I? Fifty-nine of them, actually."

"Yeah," Martin said. "A for effort, I suppose."

Zeke smiled a little half-smile.

"What was it?" Martin asked. "Your purpose? If you don't mind me asking, that is. What was your soul supposed to do on Earth? Do you remember?"

"Yeah, I do," Zeke said, closing his eyes and leaning his head back against the cavern wall again. "I was supposed to learn to put other people before myself."

"Zeke?" Zelda's eyes fluttered open. "Babe? Where am I?" She tried to sit up and failed. Martin put a hand between her shoulder blades and helped her.

"We're in a cavern, babe," Zeke said. "It's all good."

"Oh, thank God. I dreamed we went to Hell." She laughed, then winced and rubbed her temples. "Isn't that funny? And oh, I have a headache." She rested her head gingerly on Zeke's shoulder and let her eyelids droop.

"Actually," Martin said. "It's not funny at all."

Zelda opened her eyes and looked at him. "You were in my dream, too," she said. "Zeke! Zeke! He was in my dream, too."

"Cool," Zeke said. He wriggled out of his damp jacket and wrapped it around Zelda's shoulders. "You're freezing cold," he said.

"Do I even want to know why I'm soaking wet?" Zelda asked.

"Nope," Martin said.

"And what's that smell?" she said, sniffing the air and wrinkling up her face. "God, it's disgusting."

"You puked," Martin said. "You barfed all over Zeke."

"Did I really?" she asked Zeke. "What happened?"

"Yeah," he said. "You were just a little out of it for a while there, that's all. But it's OK. You're OK now." He smiled at her, relieved.

"What do you mean I was just a little out of it? What the hell happened?"

Zeke shrugged. "Nothing much, babe," he said. "Take it easy, OK?"

"Oh, God," Zelda said. "Did I, like, black out? Have a seizure? I feel really funny. Was I drooling?" She swiped at her face. "Did I do anything embarrassing?"

"That depends," Martin said with a chuckle. "On your personal threshold for humiliation. There was this plastic skeleton? And you were all like—" He was about to pantomime some of Zelda's antics when Zeke cut him off.

"Shut up, Van Assen!" Zeke said. But he chuckled a little, too. He put an arm around Zelda and rubbed her shoulder. "You were just a little sick," he told her. "It's no big deal."

"Gross," Zelda said. "I'm so sorry." She smacked her lips together a couple of times. "Anybody have a breath mint?"

"No!" Martin and Zeke both shouted at the same time. Then, they both laughed.

Zelda narrowed her eyes at the two of them. "What the hell's going on here?" she said. "Why are you friends?" She looked around at the red cavern walls and pulled Zeke's jacket tighter around herself. "And why are we sitting in this nasty cave?"

"OK," Zeke said. "About that. As I was telling Martin, the Soul Reassignment Office is aware of my attempt to return your souls to Earth, but that's as far as I can get you. Some of their guys are going to come take you the rest of the way, alright?"

"I had a dream that you weren't coming with us," Zelda said nervously.

"That's right, babe," Zeke said. "I can't. But, you can go without me. It's going to be fine. You're going to have an awesome new life, OK?"

"I want to stay with you." Zelda narrowed her eyes at him and fisted her hands at her sides, ready to fight. Then she sagged and let out her breath in a long, tired sigh. "I kind of want to yell about this," she said. "But my head is throbbing right now."

Zeke smiled at her. "Yelling won't change anything, Zel. You know you can't stay here, right? You're meant to go back. I just know it."

"Yeah," she said. "I know it, too."

Something occurred to Martin. "You're not going to lose your job over this, are you?" he asked Zeke. "I mean, if and when they find out that you helped us, won't there be repercussions?"

Zeke shrugged. "What are they gonna do? Kill me? Send me to Hell?"

"I don't know," Martin said. "Those demons on the television looked pretty sadistic. And somewhat creative, too. I imagine they could mete out some serious punishments if they were so inclined."

"Eh," Zeke said. "I'm still pretty new on the job. It'll be a first offense. I'm sure I'll just get probation or a slap on the wrist or something."

"A slap on the wrist with a hot poker by a creature with superhuman strength while suspended upside-down with your head in a vat of molten lava," Martin mumbled.

"Shut up," Zeke said. "I'll be fine."

Martin thought he looked a little bit freaked out and regretted bringing the demons into the conversation.

A rustling noise in the distance made Zeke sit up straighter. "It's almost time," he said.

"Time for what?" Martin asked.

"For you guys to go. Listen. The next patrol is about to go out."

"Patrol?"

"Yeah," Zeke said. "How do you think the demons hone in on lost souls and damnable folks just about to kick it? They've got scouts."

"Scouts?" Martin hated the way he'd felt a few beats behind Zeke ever since he'd gotten to Hell. He wondered if maybe that uncomfortable, he-knows-something-I-don't-know feeling was meant to be part of his own personal torture during his stay there.

"The bats," Zeke said.

"Of course," Martin said, nodding. "The bats. The bats out of Hell."

"Right," Zeke said. "The bats go out on regular patrols. They communicate with the demons telepathically, I think. They're rewarded with food and stuff when they locate someone the demons can snatch. They fly right through here on their way out, though, legions of them."

"Ok…?" Martin still didn't see how a patrol of scout bats was going to help him escape from Hell.

"I hate bats," Zelda said, sounding a little more like her old self. "They're totally creepy."

"Well, get over it," Zeke said. "They're your ticket out of here."

Zelda looked horrified.

"There are so many of them," Zeke said. "I can't describe it to you. You'll see. The whole cavern will be thick with them. And some of them are huge. Like, *really* big. The flying foxes have a wingspan of almost five feet."

"They sound horrible," Zelda said. "Can't we enlist the help of a demon or something instead?"

"Sorry," Zeke said bitterly. "All our little pretty boys are busy luring people to their dooms and torturing the shit out of them."

"So, the bats?" Martin said. He didn't want another Zeke-Zelda tiff to make him miss his one chance to escape.

"Yeah," Zeke said. "The bats. When they all come through here, you guys just sort of get in the middle of them, grab onto a couple of the huge ones, and soar on out of here."

Martin looked at Zeke for at least two solid minutes. He opened his mouth to say something, then closed it. He shook his head and tried again. "So, this is your big plan?" he finally managed to say.

"Yes."

"This is what you came up with?"

"Yes."

"Just to be clear, this is the big plan we've been working our way toward executing this entire time?"

"Yes."

"Your big escape plan, to summarize what I think I hear you saying, is for Zelda and me to be carried up and out of this cavern like a couple of bats out of Hell?" Martin asked slowly.

"Yes," Zeke said, clearly agitated. "Did I stutter, Fartin? That's the plan. Don't ask me again."

"Well…" Martin began.

"That plan sucks!" Zelda finished.

"Oh, OK," Zeke said. "Feel free to go ahead and come up with a better one then." He leaned back against the cavern wall again, crossed his legs at the ankles, and folded his hands behind his head. "I'll wait. I've got plenty of time. Half a millennium, at least."

The fast-approaching rustling sound made Martin and Zelda peer off into the distance.

"Better hurry and come up with your new exit strategy before anyone in the intake office comes looking for us," Zeke said. He pretended to look at his watch. "Tick-tock. The bats will be here soon."

"Alright!" Martin said. "Alright. Let's just say, hypothetically, that we were to go along with this plan. What if the bats can't carry us? What if we're too heavy for them? What if we fall?"

Zeke shrugged. "I suppose you'll be impaled on the stalagmites," he said. "But so what? I mean, it won't feel good…but you're dead, right? No real harm, no real foul."

Martin paled.

The rustling sound grew louder.

Zeke stood up and pulled Zelda to her feet. She shrugged her arms through the sleeves of his jacket and pushed them up a little. With her costume and Zeke's blazer, Martin thought, she looked like something from an eighties music video.

Martin stood up, too. He was extremely aware of being the only one there in his underwear.

"Why aren't you wearing any pants?" Zelda asked, taking notice of his predicament at last and smirking in the direction of Martin's crotch.

"Never mind that," Zeke said. "Zel, listen. I want you to know that I'm sorry, OK?"

"It's alright," she said. "They're just bats. It's only for a few minutes, right? I can handle it. I got this." She sounded like she was trying to psyche herself up. Martin wished he had half her bravado.

"No," Zeke said. "I refuse to apologize for the bats. That situation is what it is. There's no other egress you could use to get out of here. The bat idea is fucking brilliant, in fact, if I do say so myself. What I meant was, I'm sorry for everything else."

"Lila?" Zelda asked, her eyes narrowing again.

Martin was afraid she'd blow their chance of escape with one of her freak-outs.

"Yeah, OK, Lila," Zeke said. "I guess I'm sorry that I hurt you like that."

"You *guess*?"

"I'm sure, damn it! OK?" The vague rustling sound was becoming a more distinct flapping now. A little breeze stirred within the cavern. "I'm sorry for ending your life, Zelda. That's what I'm trying to say. I'm so, so sorry for cutting your Earthly life short before you fulfilled your purpose there. I'm sorry I put you through all of this. And your family…" Zeke looked like he might cry.

"Oh, babe," Zelda said. She wrapped her arms around his neck. "It's OK," she said. "It really is." Then, she kissed him with so much passion that Martin had to turn away and tug at his inadequate boxer shorts some more.

The first tiny bat flew past, and Zeke and Zelda sprang apart, then instinctively reached for each other again and held hands.

"It's time!" Zeke said. He held on tight to Zelda's hand for a few more seconds, then let it go. He stared intently into her eyes. "I love you."

"I love you, too," she said. Tears were starting to make their way down her cheeks.

"Martin," Zeke said, looking at him over the top of Zelda's head.

"Do not," Martin said. "Tell me you love me right now."

"I won't," Zeke said with a smile. "But I am sorry if I was an asshole when we first met. And, I guess, most of the time thereafter."

"If?" Martin said, as the sound of flapping bat wings grew louder all around them. "You're sorry *if* you were an asshole?"

"That," Zeke said. "OK? I'm sorry *that* I was an asshole. Is that what you want to hear, Fartin Van AssMan?"

"Worst. Apology. Ever," Martin said, but he smiled and when Zeke held out his hand, Martin shook it. He might have even said something else, but nobody would have heard him because they were suddenly overwhelmed by the arrival of a mass of swirling, flapping, squeaking bats.

"Go! Go!" Zeke was yelling. The bats were drowning out his words, but he pushed Martin and Zelda forward, toward the thick of the patrol.

Martin grabbed Zelda's hand and, without letting himself think about what they were doing, ran into the fray. They were swatted with leathery wings and scratched with sharp little claws. Small bats struck them head-on like tiny torpedoes. Martin let go of Zelda and tried to cover his head. When they were right in the middle of the horde of bats, he jumped up and grabbed hold of a big one as it flew past. He was too heavy for it, and just pulled it down toward the ground while it flapped its huge wings frantically. With his other hand he grabbed another, then threw his leg over a third. A mass of smaller bats swirled around him. His other leg found its way to a fourth big specimen.

"It's working!" Martin cried, as he started to move along with the tide of bats. He looked back over his shoulder and saw Zelda following his lead. One bat seemed to be tangled in her skirts, another in her hair, but they all bore her up and forward. The bats were so thick that if one of them dropped one of its hitchhiker's limbs, another bat was right there to take its place.

Martin watched in amazement as the cavern's red walls and spiky mineral formations sped past him. He'd never experienced an equivalent adrenaline rush on Earth. He wasn't sure he liked it. A stalactite caught on his boxers, leaving a painful gash on his lower back and exposing the top part of his rear end, and then he was positive that he hated it. He felt ridiculous, soaring through Hell with a bunch of patrol bats while his butt crack was showing, but he didn't dare let go of any of his bats to pull up his underwear, and resigned himself to arriving back on Earth partially bare-assed. It was a fitting return, he figured, for someone who had only left because of a puddle of pee and a public urinal in the first place.

Soon, the cavern disappeared behind them and the bats closed ranks to squeeze their way through a narrow, earthen tunnel. Martin looked upward, hoping to see daylight, but couldn't see anything beyond the mass of bats. His stomach, back, and thighs bumped against the sides of the tunnel, but he held on for all he was worth. He hoped to God that Zelda was doing the same behind him. He couldn't turn around to look.

Without warning, the tunnel gave way to a wide, open space. The bats fanned out, taking off in all directions, flying right out from under Martin. He felt himself falling, but it was a controlled fall, a float. He'd felt that sensation before. He knew they'd made it back to Earth. He pulled up his boxer shorts at last.

"We're ghosts again! Do you believe this?" Zelda called. A bat flapped out from under her huge skirt and flew away indignantly. Zelda, too, was in free-float. One last little bat was tangled up in her hair and she struggled to free him. As soon as they landed, Martin hurried over to help.

"Ow!" she said. Martin and the bat were both pulling her hair. Finally, the little guy was free, squealing as it flapped away. Zelda shuddered. "I'm going to have nightmares forever," she muttered.

The bats were still coming up out of the hole in the Earth by the hundreds. Martin and Zelda watched from a safe distance as they shot across the sky, a strange dark formation against a pale near-sunset backdrop. When the last stragglers finally flew out of sight, Zelda sighed and started straightening her dress. Her corset top had slipped again, and her mostly dry skirts were a dirty, twisted mess. She still wore Zeke's red jacket and dusted it off as best she could. Martin wished he had more clothes to straighten and fuss with. He tugged at his underwear self-consciously.

Zelda started smoothing her bat-teased hair. "You wouldn't happen to know what became of my crown, would you?" she asked a bit morosely.

"You threw it into the River Styx," Martin said.

"Of course I did," Zelda said. "How silly of me."

Martin looked around, took in the scenery.

"Zelda?" he said. "Do you ever get the feeling that you're going around in circles?"

Zelda glanced around them, too. "I'm not even going to waste any energy being surprised," she said. "Of course the bat-only entrance to Hell would be right in the state park where we started. Honestly, I'd be disappointed if it were anywhere else."

They were hovering above the rocky shore again, just feet from where they'd landed on Earth after sneaking through the Soul Reassignment Office's portal. Martin could see the bay lapping sweetly at the shore through Zelda's slightly transparent form.

"So, what do we do now?" Zelda asked. "Should we start walking?"

"No," Martin said. "I think we're supposed to stay put. Zeke said there would be people coming to meet us."

Zelda looked at the sky again and shivered. "Well, I hope they get here before the bats come back," she said.

The sky above them was streaked with clouds that reflected the orange glow of what must have been a truly spectacular sunset somewhere behind them. The top of the bay looked vaguely orange, too. Martin almost let it remind him of a vat of molten lava, but then he decided not to.

"It's beautiful here, right?" he said to Zelda. "Isn't it great to be back on Earth?"

Zelda shrugged. "It's not going to be Earth without Zeke. Not for me."

"He really loved you," Martin said. "That has to mean something."

"It means something," Zelda said. Martin waited for her to start crying, but she didn't. "Want to go for a walk?" she asked him.

"I don't know," Martin said. "I really think we should stick close to the bat cave to meet our escorts."

"We won't go far." Zelda had a funny gleam in her eyes that made Martin want to do whatever she asked.

"OK," he said. "Just for a minute."

Zelda grabbed his hand and led him out toward the water. Together, they took a few tentative steps off the rocks, their feet hovering above the pale orange surface of the bay.

Zelda threw her head back and laughed. "I love it!" she said. "I love that I can't touch the water here! It's like a victory over that lake we drove into." She looked sad for a second, then she smiled again. She stomped her foot, but the surface of the water was undisturbed. "Ha!" she laughed, and ran out deeper, pulling Martin along with her.

Martin looked back over his shoulder a little nervously, expecting to see the folks from the Soul Reassignment

Office watching disapprovingly from the shore, but there were no navy suits in sight. He looked out over the water again and smiled. He and Zelda hurtled past the tiny little breakers to the calmer water where the day's last light made everything feel surreal.

"I'm going to miss this," Zelda said.

Martin knew she meant her Earthly life and everything in it. Maybe she even meant the invincible feeling of being a ghost in the physical world, and the beauty they had found in that world since they'd died, but he let himself imagine she might have meant something else, too. "Me, too," he told her. "I'm going to miss this, too."

They stood over the water together for a few more minutes, absorbing the last of the day's Earthly beauty, then turned back toward shore. Martin scanned the rocks there, starting to worry. "Shouldn't someone have met us by now?" he wondered aloud to Zelda.

Zelda was still smiling a dreamy little smile, watching the water pass inches beneath her feet as they walked. Martin had his arm around her and she leaned against his shoulder with a sigh. "I don't know," she said. "But, as I recall, those dudes from the Soul Reassignment Office don't seem to have a problem with making people wait."

"That's true," Martin said. But he couldn't help wondering whether something had gone wrong. What if Zeke had misunderstood? What if nobody were coming to meet them? Then they'd be trapped on Earth as a couple of verloren again.

They reached the rocky shore, and Zelda went to sit/hover on a small boulder. It was getting darker fast, and Martin squinted up and down the shoreline, looking for any sign of afterlife civil servants. Finally, he pointed off into the distance. "Someone's coming!" he said. "I think it's a couple of Seekers!"

Zelda stood up, too. She peered at the two figures approaching. "I think you're right," she said. "Hey!" she yelled, waving her arms. "Over here!"

One of the distant figures waved back, acknowledging them.

"We're saved!" Zelda yelled gleefully, throwing herself into Martin's arms. He caught her and gave her a squeeze, then set her back down. "Zeke did it!" she said. She sounded happy and sad at the same time. "He really did it."

"We owe him one," Martin said, grabbing Zelda's hand. "Come on."

He started pulling her in the direction of the Seekers in their navy suits. One of them was speaking into some kind of small phone or walkie-talkie. They both strode toward Martin and Zelda quickly, looking extremely serious. "Uh oh," Martin said quietly, before the Seekers were in earshot. "They look a little pissed off. I think we might be in some trouble."

"Crap," Zelda said, slowing her pace.

Behind them, there was an explosion of sound. Martin had never heard anything like it. Later, in his memory of it, he might be able to pick out screams, roars, wingbeats, and fiery eruptions, but on the shoreline in the semi-darkness, it was all just a big cacophony of evil noise.

The two Seekers broke into a run, headed straight for Martin and Zelda. The one with the radio was screaming frantically into it.

Something told Martin not to look back, but he didn't listen. He turned to face the source of the terrifying sound, and saw five huge demons coming after them. These demons hadn't bothered with the pretense of their supermodel forms. Their claws were out, both literally and figuratively. They were black-skinned, red-eyed behemoths, at least three times the size of Martin. Spikes protruded from their arms and legs, huge black wings bore them through the air. They were ready for battle, and, comparatively, Martin and Zelda made poorly armed opponents.

"Demons!" Martin called to Zelda, just in case pointing out the obvious would improve their situation. It didn't.

"Run!"

They stumbled forward a few steps, but there were still at least fifty yards between them and the Seekers who might have been able to help. Martin seriously doubted that a couple of navy suits and a walkie-talkie were going to be much of a match for the claws and spikes of their pursuers. He heard the demons' wingbeats right behind them, felt the breezes they were churning up in the air. He grabbed Zelda and hurled her to the ground, where they hovered together. Martin covered her with his body as best he could, bracing for whatever agony the hellish beasts decided to inflict on him first.

As Martin squeezed his eyes shut tight, another huge sound shook the air all around him. He counted to five, made sure he wasn't about to be ripped to smithereens, then chanced a glance behind him.

An ethereal white light illuminated the entire shoreline now, and the beasts from Hell were being driven back by an army of white creatures swooping through the sky. The men in navy finally reached Martin and Zelda. "Are you alright?" one of them yelled, out of breath, but he didn't wait for an answer. "Don't worry. We're going to get you out of here! STAT!"

Martin and Zelda got clumsily to their feet, but neither of them could tear their eyes away from the sky. More and more of the white creatures swooped in. They were almost reptilian, with shimmering iridescent scales covering their muscled bodies and huge, white, glistening wings like the dragons of childhood fairy tales. They were smaller than the demons, but easily overpowered them with their numbers. A disembodied black arm terminating in a clawed hand hurtled past Martin and Zelda in flames. Zelda jumped back and Martin pulled her close, tried to shield her from the sight of it with his body.

"What's happening?" Martin shouted past Zelda to the man with the walkie-talkie, who was looking at his watch.

"The demons!" the man yelled back over the din. "They're trying to take you back to Hell!"

"And the other guys?" Martin shouted.

"We had to call in some reinforcements," the man yelled back. "Angels." He looked at his watch again. "Don't worry," he said. "We should be able to get a portal open here soon."

"Angels?" Martin looked in awe at the war being waged above him. "Zelda," he said. "Look!" He knew his voice was catching, but he didn't care. "Zelda, they sent angels to help us. Angels! To help *us*!"

Cautiously, Zelda chanced a glance at the sky. "They're beautiful," she breathed.

Even the men in navy were staring up at the sky. Martin figured that even on The Other Side, this type of clash wasn't an everyday occurrence.

"Heaven and Hell are locked in an epic battle for our souls right now," Zelda said. "Should we really just be standing here? Shouldn't we do something?"

"Uhm…" Martin looked around. A fragment of singed demon wing fluttered to Earth near their feet. Just above them, two angels teamed up against one of the angrier-looking demons.

Martin reached into the pocket of his Honor Society sweatshirt and pulled out *Soul Reassignment Procedures and Policies: A Manual*. He chucked it at the furious demon nearest him as hard as he could. It bounced off the monster's thick skin and tumbled back to the ground, out of Martin's reach. The demon didn't even flinch. Martin felt his face redden. For about the millionth time, he wished he at least had the dignity afforded by a pair of pants.

"Let me try," Zelda said. She reached up under her skirt and unsheathed her rubber dagger.

"Miss?" one of the men in navy said, reaching out to stop her.

His partner held him back. "Let her have her fun," he said. "She's not going to hurt anything." He checked his watch again and frowned.

Zelda chucked the prop dagger at the demon, who didn't even notice it bouncing off his knee. Several more angels swooped in to join the fight, and the howling beast from Hell was silenced for all eternity as they ripped his fierce-looking head off and it burst into flames.

Zelda made a gagging noise and turned away.

"Eh," Martin said. "We tried."

Chapter 17

The battle between good and evil was wrapping up. Only one demon remained intact, but he was grappling with about a dozen of the shimmering, reptilian-looking angels and clearly didn't stand a chance. All along the rocky shore, pieces of defeated demons smoldered and smoked. Martin kept scanning the sky, but he didn't see any fiendish reinforcements on the way. The magnificent angels, though, kept coming in droves. The sky was almost completely obscured by them. The otherworldly white light they'd brought with them stretched as far as Martin's ghostly eye could see.

A couple of the angels landed near where Martin and Zelda stood with the Seekers. "Any word on the portal?" one of them asked. "We should get these souls to safety." His voice was like music. Martin couldn't tear his gaze away from the angel's face. His eyes were snake-like, unblinking, but perfectly, serenely blue. Martin wanted to swim in them. Zelda must have felt similarly. She leaned toward the angels and stared at them in wonder.

"Some kind of a SNAFU," the Seeker with the radio said. "All the passcodes were just changed and they can't get the new access card readers to work. Waiting for a portal back to the regional branch is like waiting for Satan to take a snow day right now."

"It's a shitshow at our office lately," his partner said. "Pardon my French, but these new security measures they've put in place are killing us."

Martin cringed.

"We can take them for you if you want," one of the angels offered, pointing toward Martin and Zelda. "We have been ordered to fall back anyway." He looked up at the sky, then at the beach littered with demon remains. "There is not much left to do here but clean up now." He wrinkled his face a little where Martin thought a nose should have been, but wasn't.

"Yeah, OK," the first guy in navy said. "That'd be great."

"Can you take all of us, actually?" the other one asked. "I don't know about my partner here, but I've got better things to do than wait around on the physical plane all day for some flunkie to troubleshoot the portal regulator."

"Of course," the angel said. He looked skyward and, with no visible or audible sign, got the attention of two of his fellow celestial beings, who drifted gracefully to Earth and landed next to him.

"We are happy to help," one of the new arrivals said. The other nodded in agreement.

Martin was duly impressed. Telepathy. Looks. Immense strength. These angels really had it all.

"Alright, then, let's get going," the navy suit with the radio in his hand said. "Thanks a million," he told the angel nearest him, holding out his hand for a handshake. "We owe you one."

The angel grasped his hand warmly and laughed. He clapped him on the back like an old friend. "I shall have Our Father put it on your tab."

The navy suits split up. Each of them climbed onto the back of an angel, having no apparent qualms about riding piggyback on agents of God Almighty himself.

Martin was much more self-conscious.

"We'll see you back at the office," one of the Seekers said to the rest of the group. "No funny business," he told Martin and Zelda, pointing a finger at them over his angel's shoulder. "I mean it."

"Watch these two," the other Seeker told the remaining angels, resting a hand on the shoulder of the heavenly being closest to him. "They're known flight risks."

"Have faith," the angel said calmly. "There will not be any trouble." He looked up and smiled beatifically. The last demon was being dismembered now and the crowd in the sky had thinned out considerably. "It is a glorious day, with two lost souls reclaimed. Let us focus on the joy in that."

"I'll try," the Seeker said, but he didn't sound very joyful. "Let's just get going."

The angels, bearing the men in navy on their backs, rose up into the air while Martin and Zelda watched, fascinated and terrified.

"Come," one of the other angels said in his melodic voice. He reached an iridescent hand toward Martin and Zelda.

"Uhm," Martin said uncomfortably as a blob of burning demon flesh landed just to his right. "I had to give up my pants." It really sounded dumb, he thought, when you didn't have time to tell the story right.

The angel smiled. "I know," he said. "You do not need them. Come."

The angels boosted a shy, pantsless Martin and an open-mouthed Zelda onto their backs.

"Amazing!" Zelda said, laughing with delight. "Unreal! So, it's all true, then? Heaven, God, angels...the whole bit?"

"The whole bit," her angel answered.

"Can we go there?" Zelda wanted to know. "To Heaven?"

"Maybe," the angel told her. "In time."

"Now, we have to get back to the Soul Reassignment Office without further delay," the other angel said. "Are you both ready?"

Martin and Zelda nodded.

"Hang on," the angel said, and took off into the sky.

The flight was smoother than Martin had anticipated. The angels' big wings made fluid motions through the air. Martin gripped his angel around its smooth, iridescent neck for all he was worth, holding him in a virtual headlock, but Zelda wrapped her legs around her angel's waist and threw her hands up into the air.

"This is so much better than bats!" she cried happily as her long red skirts blew backward in the wind and her hair streamed out behind her. Martin felt like he was watching two angels when he looked over at her and her heavenly partner flying alongside him. He loosened his grip on his own angel's windpipe and relaxed a little.

Martin was disappointed to see an office tower looming ahead of them just as he was starting to enjoy his angelback ride. The angels landed on the roof at a run, slowed to a walk, then stopped. Martin and Zelda climbed down, Martin making sure his boxer shorts were still covering the most crucial parts of his body. Zelda threw her arms around her angel's neck and whispered her thanks into the place where an ear might have been if he'd been human.

Martin looked at his own angel and held out his hand awkwardly. "Uh, thanks for the lift," he said.

"You are welcome," the angel told him, grasping Martin's hand in both of his and bowing ever so slightly.

"So, uh. Do you know how we're supposed to get in?" Martin asked, peering over the edge of the building's roof. He really hoped he wasn't supposed to rappel or anything. He'd definitely had enough adventures for one afterlifetime.

"There," his angel said, pointing to a little maintenance door across the rooftop. He smiled. "All they talk about around here are their new security measures, but that door is never locked. It will take you where you need to go."

"Thank you again," Martin said.

"Pleasant journeys," the angel replied.

"Goodbye," Martin said.

"I love you!" Zelda cried.

The angels smiled. "We love you, too," the one Zelda had ridden on said, and the whole rooftop felt suddenly warm with the sincerity of the sentiment. "I hope we will meet again someday under less urgent circumstances."

The sleek, powerful angels turned and rose back into the sky. They took their beautiful white light with them, and Martin and Zelda were left standing in the semi-darkness of early evening.

Martin had that weird feeling he used to have as a boy when his sweet Grandma Van Assen used to come for a long visit and then leave, taking all the extra hugs, cuddles, and fun away with her. He looked over at Zelda. She must have felt it, too. Tears streamed silently down her face.

Chapter 18

Zelda put a hand on Martin's arm. They watched the angels go until they had flown out of sight, then Martin led Zelda toward the little door in the rooftop. She kept looking back over her shoulder, as if she hoped the angels might reappear.

Martin half-expected the door to be locked after all, just because nothing about his time as one of the verloren had gone at all according to plan, but, to his surprise, the door swung open easily when he pulled on the handle.

"After you," he said to Zelda, stepping aside.

Zelda peered through the doorway. It appeared to lead to a plain, fluorescently lit stairwell. She hesitated.

"Together," she said. She took Martin's hand and they crossed the threshold. The door swung slowly shut behind them, closing with a thud. Martin and Zelda both stood stock still, waiting for something to happen. Martin supposed they'd both become accustomed to expecting the unexpected since their Earthly lives had ended.

"Huh," Martin said when nothing unusual happened. "Do you think we're just supposed to walk down the stairs to the reception area? Why does that seem too easy?"

"I don't know," Zelda said trepidatiously. She leaned forward just a little bit and peeked over the stairway railing. "I'm a little leery of heading downstairs since our time in you-know-where."

Martin chuckled. "We've actually gone to Hell," he said in disbelief.

"To Hell and back," Zelda corrected him.

"So I think we can handle one staircase."

Zelda sighed. "OK," she said. "On the count of three. One. Two. Th—"

Martin took a step forward just as Zelda counted three and felt his sneaker-clad foot sink into a familiar plasma-like substance. "Hang on!" he tried to yell as he and Zelda tumbled through the invisible, thick goo that had first welcomed him to the Soul Reassignment Office following his accident in the public restroom. It was just as disorienting as the first trip through it, except he was even more aware of the plasma around him this time because he wasn't wearing pants. Martin and Zelda landed together on the cheap carpeting just outside RECEPTION AND WAITING. The two Seekers in navy suits were waiting for them and hurried over.

"We've got them," one of the Seekers said, talking into his radio. "Van Assen and Kozikowski are in the building. Over."

"Copy that," someone answered through a little bit of static. "Operation Beat the Heat complete. Over."

"Operation Beat the Heat?" Zelda said with a smirk, raising a snarky eyebrow at the guy holding the walkie-talkie.

"Hey," he said. "I don't name 'em. We leave that to the man upstairs."

"God?" Martin was disappointed, honestly. He would have thought the all-knowing, all-powerful God could have come up with a much better, far less cheesy code name for their rescue mission.

"No," the Seeker said, annoyed. "Not God. Joel Remington." He pointed to his walkie-talkie, indicating the person on the other end. "He works upstairs. In the Office of Lost Soul Recovery."

"Oh," Martin said. "Of course."

"Give the guy a break, alright? He's working with a skeleton crew as it is and everyone's been gunning twenty-four seven on your case."

"Right," Martin said. "Thanks for that, by the way."

Zelda tilted her head to one side. "By skeleton crew," she said. "Do you mean, like, actual skeletons or—"

"That's enough chit-chat, huh? Let's get 'em processed," the other Seeker said. "We're gonna have a shitload of paperwork to get through before we can put this one to bed, and I ain't trying to put in any more overtime than I have to."

"Amen," his partner said. He turned to Martin and Zelda. "You heard the man. Let's go."

Martin and Zelda got to their feet and let the Seekers usher them through the frosted-glass doors at the end of the corridor. Martin had an overwhelming sense of déjà vu. He wondered whether that was what it had been like for Zeke to walk through those same doors fifty-nine different times.

Martin recognized the receptionist sitting behind the desk from his first visit to the office. She looked just as sweet as she had then, but when she saw them her expression definitely soured.

"Well, look who it is," the receptionist said as they approached her desk and the frosted-glass entry doors disappeared, becoming a solid wall behind them. A new sign was hanging there now, a chalkboard on which someone had written, "Days Without Escapees: 09."

"My, my. The prodigal souls return," the receptionist continued. "Welcome back."

Martin wasn't one-hundred percent sure, but he thought she didn't really mean it. He stared longingly at the coffee maker on the counter above her desk. He knew it wouldn't taste good, but it had been so long since he'd had even a poor substitute for coffee that he found himself starting to salivate.

"You two have caused me a lot of trouble," the receptionist said. "And where's your other friend? Our frequent flyer? He doesn't deign to grace us with his presence again?"

"Affirmative," the Seeker closest to Martin said. "It's just these two at present."

"Fine," the receptionist said. She noticed Martin eyeing her coffee maker. She reached up and took a big stack of foam cups off the counter and shoved them into her desk drawer. "No coffee today," she said, looking right at him. "We're fresh out of cups."

The Seekers tried to hide their chuckles.

"Well, I think you're in good hands here," one of them said to Martin, suppressing a smile and clapping him heartily on the shoulder. His radio crackled in his pocket. "This is where we leave you."

"OK," Martin said a little morosely. "And, listen, thanks for everything. Really."

"Yes, thank you," Zelda said. "We're truly grateful."

The Seekers nodded at them a bit curtly and headed off down the hall without another word.

The receptionist came out from behind her desk, her arms full of paperwork. She handed Martin and Zelda each a clipboard with a Soul Reassignment Office pen attached. "I trust you kept your manuals?" she said.

Zelda looked away.

"It was the darndest thing," Martin said. "There were these demons, see, and—"

"Uh huh," the receptionist said, eyebrows raised. She leaned over the counter behind her and picked up two more manuals. She handed one to each of them. "No problem," she said. "Just take another one. It's not like they're expensive to produce. It's not like if I run out, they make me go all the way down to the basement and bring up another super-heavy box full of them all by myself. Manuals for navigating the soul reassignment process grow on trees, right? Here," she said, grabbing another handful and tossing them at Martin and Zelda. "Come to think of it, just take a bunch."

The manuals fell around their feet. Zelda looked at Martin with wide eyes.

"Uh, thanks," Martin said, stooping to pick up the little books. He gathered them and stacked them on the reception counter. "I think we'll just stick with the one copy." Martin glanced at the stack of books and saw that their plain white covers all read, *Soul Reassignment Procedures and Policies: A Manual REVISED EDITION* in plain black type.

"Suit yourself," the receptionist huffed. She knelt at Zelda's feet and started lifting up her skirt.

"Hey!" Zelda yelled, stepping backward and pulling her dress tight around her. "What do you think you're doing?"

The receptionist gave them both an exasperated look. She held something small and black up for them to see. "Ankle monitor?" she said, thoroughly annoyed. "Everyone without an appointment has to wear one now." She reached for Zelda's ankle again, with more success. "You're next, Mr. Underpants," she said.

Martin flinched as the cold tracking device touched his bare skin. "I can assure you this isn't necessary," Martin said.

"If you don't like it—and I wouldn't blame you if you hated it—take it up with this bunch of jerks we had through here a little while ago," the receptionist said, glowering up at him. She finished affixing the monitor and stood up. "Took it upon themselves to slip out right under my nose."

"Actually," Zelda said. "You were nowhere in sight when we took off the last time."

"I have a lot to do around here!" the receptionist said, leaning toward Zelda angrily. "I do the jobs of, like, at least three people. Everything that nobody else wants to do, they push off on me. I'm supposed to guard the souls in transition, too? Give me a break."

"We're really sorry," Martin said.

"You're *sorry*? I got chewed out by every higher-up in this organization over your little disappearing act! And it was just before review time, too, so guess who's not getting a performance-based bonus this year?"

"We're really very sorry for any trouble we might have caused you," Martin tried again. "We didn't think—"

"No," the receptionist snapped. "I guess you didn't." She smoothed her skirt and took a deep breath. "This way to the new-and-improved waiting room."

Wait for It

The plain glass WAITING door was gone. In its place was a high-tech, double-paned sliding model reinforced with a layer of chicken wire between its glass panels. The receptionist used her swipe card to open it for them. Across the hall, where a heavily trafficked portal back to Earth had once opened and closed on a regular basis, a big Out of Order sign now hung. A huge X made out of yellow and black caution tape warned people away from the area. Inside the waiting room, a bored-looking security guard sat on a stool just inside the door, flipping through what looked like a celebrity gossip rag. He looked up from the magazine when Martin and Zelda entered, then went back to reading.

"Have a seat and fill out your paperwork," the receptionist said. "Someone will be with you shortly. Or whenever I get around to calling them." She laughed. "In the meantime, can I get you anything to make your stay more comfortable?"

"Uh, a bottle of water would be great," Zelda said. "Thanks."

"Coffee?" Martin asked, folding his hands prayerfully in front of him and begging. "Please?"

"Coming right up," the receptionist said.

"Really?" Martin said enthusiastically. "Thanks!"

"No, not really," she said with a sneer. "And smile, OK? You're on camera." She pointed to a camera and monitor suspended from the ceiling before she left and the door slid shut behind her with a very loud click.

"Oh, God, I look awful!" Zelda moaned, stepping closer to the security monitor. She tried to smooth her hair and fluff her skirt a little.

Martin stared morosely through the waiting-room door at the signage on the wall where the portal had once been in use. He thought he might finally have figured out where it all went wrong for him. Just as he was warming up for a nice bit of brooding, the receptionist strutted by the glass sliding door with a big foam cup in her hand. She stopped right in front of Martin, took a sip from it, and shuddered and rolled her eyes heavenward in ecstasy. Then, she smiled and waved at Martin and disappeared again.

Martin gazed after the receptionist and sighed. Then, he jumped back in alarm as a guy not much older than he was threw himself up against the glass door with an enthusiastic *thwap*. The kid smiled and fumbled for an access card that hung from a lanyard around his neck and opened up the door.

"Is it really true?" he asked gleefully, looking at Martin in amazement. "Are you really Van Assen?" He looked over Martin's shoulder to where Zelda was still studying her hair in the security-camera image. "And Kozikowski?"

"Um, yes?" Martin answered, taking a step back and pulling his sweatshirt down self-consciously. "That's us."

"I can't believe it!" the kid said, his eyes wide. He reached out to shake Martin's hand. "I'm Steve. Steven Wright. I'm an intern here, upstairs. I can't believe I'm meeting you! You're, like, totally famous around here."

Zelda snorted. "Yeah," she said, turning away from the security footage of herself. "They're giving us the real celebrity treatment." She held out her ankle monitor for Steve to inspect.

"Well," Steve said. "I know some people are pretty pissed at you, and—don't get me wrong—you sure caused everyone a whole lot of trouble, but I think it was a total rock-star move to sneak through the portal like that and make it back here to tell the tale."

"Thanks," Martin said. "We owe everyone here who helped rescue us an awful lot of credit, though."

"I helped!" Steve shouted.

"You did?" Zelda asked, raising an eyebrow at him.

"Well, yeah." Steve puffed out his chest a little. "I taped over the portal." He gestured toward the out-of-order door across the hallway. "The caution tape? That was all me!"

As if on cue, a corner of the caution tape came unstuck and fluttered pathetically toward the floor.

"Great job," Zelda said, turning back to study herself in the TV. "Really excellent work there."

Steve deflated a little.

"Maybe you'd better be moving along now, Steve," the security guard suggested kindly, but firmly. "Isn't Mr. Remington expecting you back upstairs?"

"Oh," Steve said. "Yeah. Right. Listen." He turned to Martin again. "Can I do anything for you before I go?" he asked. "Get you anything while you wait?"

Martin almost asked for pants or suggested Steve pull some strings to get him a plum assignment in his next life, but then he got his priorities in order. "Coffee," he said, folding his hands and pleading. "Please, *please* bring me a cup of coffee."

"Coming right up!" Steve looked jubilant and purposeful as he hustled out of the waiting room.

The security guard chuckled to himself and turned a page in his magazine.

Martin waited with anticipation for Steve to reappear with a nice hot cup of anything even remotely coffee-like, but his hopes of a warm beverage were dashed when, moments later, Steve reappeared being dragged down the hallway by the furious receptionist; she had his access-card lanyard in her grasp and was using it like a leash. The receptionist narrowed her eyes at Martin and shook her head in disgust as she stormed past.

"Sorry," Steve mouthed as he was dragged past the glass waiting-room door.

Martin stared after them a minute, then he let his breath out in an indignant little huff and sat down to complete his paperwork. At least he knew some of the answers this time. Zelda finally gave up on her primping and sat down next to him. Martin was pleased to see her actually trying to fill out her forms like a good little soul. She chewed the end of her pen in consternation. Martin thought it was absolutely adorable.

"You're amazing," Martin said to her, surprising himself a little.

"Don't distract me, Van Assen," Zelda said with a little smile. "I'm trying to get my paperwork done here."

"I know," Martin said. "I'm sorry. I just wanted to be sure I got a chance to tell you before…"

"Yeah," Zelda said. "OK. You've amazed me a few times, too."

"Thanks," Martin said.

They both went back to filling out their forms.

Martin stopped writing and reached for Zelda's hand.

"No funny business," the security guard said, looking at them over the top of his magazine.

Martin let go of Zelda's hand.

"What did you put for number twenty-two on Form 3A?" he asked her.

Zelda flipped through her forms. "'What is your idea of the perfect assignment?'" she read. "I put, 'Even-tempered blonde woman with a tiny waist and an aptitude for playing the harp.'"

"The harp?" Martin asked.

Zelda shrugged. "I've always wanted to learn. What about you? What are you hoping for the next time around?"

"I can't decide," Martin said, truthfully. "I mean, I was really into being Martin Van Assen. I guess I'll just write that." Martin's pen scratched away.

"Do you think they give you what you want?" Zelda asked. "Do you think they take these answers into consideration when they pick our next assignments?"

"I don't know," Martin said.

Zelda looked toward the waiting room door and frowned. "If Ms. Secretary has anything to say about it, I'm going to have to go back as a cross-eyed dwarf with a skin condition." Zelda shuddered.

Martin laughed a little, but he didn't find it that funny. He'd been thinking the same thing. He'd had it way too easy in his last life, he knew that. That's why he'd been spoiled enough to think the rules of soul reassignment didn't have to apply to him. He fully expected to be taken down a peg or two in his next life. He tried to embrace the idea of overcoming whatever challenges awaited him instead of fearing them, but he wasn't entirely successful.

"They're going to separate us, right?" Zelda said. "Like in grade school when the teacher always made you sit apart from your best friends to minimize talking and mischief in class?"

"For our own good," Martin said, nodding. "I guess that makes sense. I really don't know."

"I wish Zeke were here," Zelda said, her voice heavy with emotion. "He seemed to know everything."

"About Zeke," Martin said a little awkwardly. "He wanted me to tell you something."

Zelda sat up straighter.

"Even if he does ever go back to Earth—and he's assured me that he doesn't plan to—he won't be able to remember his past lives anymore. So, he can't come looking for you, Zelda. He wanted you to know."

Zelda was quiet. The kind of quiet where she didn't even exhale for a while. "Damn," she finally said softly. "I guess I'd actually been sort of hoping for that."

"I'm sorry," Martin said.

Zelda sighed. "It's OK. I wouldn't have recognized him anyway, right?" She blinked hard a few times. "And it's better for him this way, isn't it? All those lives he'd lived were torturing him."

Martin nodded.

"Do you think they caught him?" Zelda asked. "The demons or whoever? Do you think they know he helped us escape?"

Probably, Martin thought. "Nah," he said. "Zeke's smart. I'm sure he covered his tracks."

Zelda nodded and pulled Zeke's red blazer tighter around her.

"I know you and I probably won't remember each other either," Zelda said. "But I'm going to try."

Martin smiled. "I'll try, too. Somewhere, on some level, you're entirely unforgettable, Zelda Kozikowski."

"Maybe we'll find each other again," she said. "Do you think that's possible?"

"After everything we've seen," Martin said. "I think anything's possible. I'll keep my eye out for a cross-eyed dwarf with a skin condition. OK?"

"Alright," Zelda said, smiling. "And I'll be on the lookout for an uptight academic bowl geek in his underwear."

Martin laughed. "They've *got* to give me pants when I get back to Earth. Wait. I'm adding that to my form." He quickly inked in "pants-wearing" next to his answer to question twenty-two on Form 3A.

Zelda went back to her paperwork. Martin sighed and did the same. He actually answered every question. It was a really good feeling to finally be proud of his work on an assignment in his post-Earthly existence. While he waited for Zelda to wrap up her own paperwork, he picked up the revised edition of the manual and flipped through it.

"Look at this." He nudged Zelda. "There's a whole new chapter in here about security procedures."

"What does it say?" she asked.

"Well, for one thing? These ankle monitors? They're also hooked up to some kind of invisible fence system. We'll be shocked into a state of paralysis if we try to leave the building."

"Ouch," Zelda said.

"We're even mentioned!" Martin said. "Though not by name. It says, 'Following the escape of several rogue souls after millennia of perfect compliance, we regret to inform our new arrivals that they are subject to searches, restraints, and confinement at the discretion of our staff.' How awesome is that?"

"I guess they let us off easy by just taking away the coffee cups, huh?" Zelda said.

"And, look," Martin said. "They're supposed to issue us a phone, so we can call the office for help if we somehow manage to escape and get into trouble."

"Huh," Zelda said. "That really would have saved us from a world of hurt."

"The cell phone program's been discontinued," the security guard said.

"Excuse me?" Martin said. He'd almost forgotten that they were being watched.

"I said they stopped handing out the phones," the guard said. "You're not going to get one."

"How come?" Zelda asked.

"Something to do with Satan," the guard said with a shrug. "He hacked our database, got all the numbers. He was texting people, I guess. Trying to convince them to break out of here like you three had done so his guys could sweep in and claim their souls."

"Wow," Martin said. "Did he get many souls that way?"

"No," the security guard told them with a snort. "I mean, what kind of text message would he have had to send folks to make them actually want to wander the Earth as one of the verloren? Seriously, under what conditions could that possibly seem like a good idea? If you've read so much as the table of contents of the manual, you'd know better than to—" The security guard stopped talking and looked at them. "No offense," he said.

"None taken," Martin said with a sigh. He quickly added "less susceptible to peer pressure" to his answer for question twenty-two on Form 3A.

Some official-looking types passing the waiting area stopped and peered in at Martin and Zelda through the glass of the sliding door. One of them pointed and said something to another. All of them shook their heads before they moved on.

"Is that overzealous intern the only person here who doesn't hate us?" Martin asked nobody in particular, trying to pull his boxer shorts lower to cover a little more of his thighs.

"I know, right?" Zelda said. "I never saw myself as a pariah. Do you think it suits me?" She turned her head from side to side, modeling her pariahness for Martin.

"Yeah," Martin said with a smile. "You wear it well."

"They don't all hate you," the security guard said, closing his magazine and tossing it onto an end table.

"I don't know," Martin told him. "The receptionist is definitely holding a grudge."

"Oh, Renata?" The security guard laughed. "She's elevated grudge-holding to an art form. Believe me, I should know." He winked. "But, most people I've talked to around here are just curious about you, that's all. Your disappearance caused quite a commotion, you know? I can't remember the last time they convened a special task force. You're pretty famous, at least around this office. My buddies aren't gonna believe me when I tell them I got to guard your asses." He laughed.

"Pariah, object of curiosity, whatever," Zelda said, slumping down in her chair. "You know what? I just want to get out of here. I'm ready to go." She held her clipboard up toward the security camera. "I'm doooooone!" she yelled.

"Take it easy," Martin told her, gently lowering her clipboard back onto her lap. "Let's not get impatient and do anything rash. Again."

The receptionist, Renata, arrived and opened the sliding door.

"Reginald," she said to the security officer with a curt nod.

"Renata," he said with a small smile and a twinkle in his eye.

"I trust these two have been behaving themselves?"

"Oh, yeah," the security guard said. "No problems whatsoever."

"Good," Renata said. She turned to Martin and Zelda. "Paperwork?" she said, eyebrows raised.

"Yes, ma'am," Martin said, gathering up both his and Zelda's clipboards. He felt a little pang of sadness as his eyes fell on his name in print for the last time. *Goodbye, Martin Van Assen. Hello...?* Martin sighed and handed both clipboards to the receptionist. "Oh," he said. "And here are our pens, too. Ma'am."

Zelda made a little sucking-up sound behind him.

Renata looked over their forms, then looked back at them. "Very nice work," she said, a little grudgingly. "Thank you."

"No problem," Martin said. He nudged Zelda with his knee.

"Yeah," Zelda said. "No sweat."

Renata looked over the forms briefly again, pausing once in a while and chewing the inside of her cheek as she re-read some of their answers. "OK," she said. "This shouldn't take too much longer now." She pursed her lips and sighed. "Would you like some coffee while you wait?" she asked Martin. "I think we just got a new shipment of cups."

"Thank you," Martin said. "That'd be awesome. Really."

"OK. Just give me a sec." Renata left and the door slid shut behind her.

"She likes you," Zelda said. Did she sound jealous?

"I thought she hated me," Martin said. "I'm a little bit afraid to see what she brings me to drink."

Renata returned momentarily with a big steaming cup of tasteless I Can't Believe It's Coffee and handed it to Martin.

"Thank you," he said again.

"Uh huh," Renata said. "Let me go get the rest of your paperwork started. We'll have you out of here in a jiffy."

She turned to go, then stopped and looked at Martin again. "Can I ask you something?" she said.

Martin had just burned his tongue on his scorching-hot, flavorless beverage. He tried to say, "Sure," but it came out more like, "Suh!"

"How did you come up with your answer to question sixty-five on Form 4?"

"Sorry," Martin said, his tongue smarting. "Which question was that?"

"'What, in your opinion, is the most important thing your soul could do during the course of your next Earthly life?'" Renata reminded him. "You wrote down, 'To learn to find the meaning in the mundane.' Were you quoting someone?"

"Uh, no," Martin said. "I was just…guessing, I guess."

"Oh," Renata said. She looked kind of disappointed. "It's a good answer, anyway. Most people just leave that one blank or write something cheesy about helping their fellow men," she said, and left.

"Nerd," Zelda said with a sneer.

"OK," Martin said. "What did you put down for that one?"

Zelda shrugged.

"Oh, come on," Martin said. "You wrote down the one thing you hope to accomplish during your next life on Earth and now you forget what you said it was? Bullshit."

"Alright," she said. "Fine. You want to know what I wrote? I wrote, 'Help my fellow men.' OK? I thought the best goal to pursue while living in the physical world might be to find ways to help others. Like how Zeke helped us. And the angels. And those Seeker guys. OK, Van Assen? OK?"

"Yeah," Martin said. "OK. It's a good answer."

"Not good enough to warrant something to drink, apparently," Zelda muttered. "Maybe I should strip down to my panties."

Martin felt his face get hot. He shifted around in his chair some more, trying to find a way to make his boxer shorts be pants.

Zelda started picking at her cuticles. Martin was bored enough to watch her. When she made herself bleed a little, she stuck her finger in her mouth.

The sliding door opened and a woman in a tailored pants suit stepped in. "Kozikowski?" she said, sounding uncertain about the pronunciation. "Zelda Kozikowski?"

"That's me," Zelda said. She jumped up out of her seat. She turned to Martin with wide eyes. "That's me!" she repeated. He thought he saw her upper lip trembling just a little bit.

Martin stood up, too. "It's alright," he said. "This is what we've been waiting for, right?"

Zelda nodded, then threw herself into Martin's arms. He squeezed her tight, corset and all.

"OK," Zelda said, pulling away from him. "OK." She swiped at her eyes and stood up straight. "I'm going now."

"Pleasant journeys," Martin said.

Zelda smiled. "You, too," she said. "Maybe I'll see you on the flip side, huh?"

"Maybe."

"Ms. Kozikowski? Are you ready to go?" The woman in the pants suit smiled patiently.

Zelda turned to face her. "I was born ready," she said confidently. Then, she faltered a little. "I mean, I'm ready to be born? Whatever. Let's just go."

The woman in the pants suit held the door open.

"See ya, Van Assen," Zelda called over her shoulder.

Martin held up a hand in a farewell gesture as Zelda followed the woman in the pants suit out of the waiting room and the door slid shut behind them.

The security guard was giving Martin a funny look. He realized he was still standing there with his hand up, so he lowered it, cleared his throat a couple of times, and sat back down. He crossed one ankle over his other knee, then decided that was a bad move for a guy in his underwear. He sat with his knees together, wondering when it would be his turn to take on a new assignment. And a new pair of pants.

A few more people passed the fish-bowl-like waiting area and peeked in at Martin, a pantsless soul in captivity. When Renata walked by again, he thought he saw her wink. The security guard must have noticed it as well. He sprang up from his stool and opened the sliding door.

"Hey, Rennie," he called. "Rennie! Wait up!" He stepped out of the waiting area and Martin could see him chatting up the beautiful receptionist just outside the door.

For the first time since his ill-fated trip to the public restroom at the Cineplex 2000 an entire afterlifetime ago, Martin Van Assen found himself completely and utterly alone. He sipped his now-tepid coffee. He took a deep breath and let it out slowly. Then he did it again, not because he needed the oxygen, but because it just felt good to let himself breathe.

He leaned his head back against the wall and crossed his ankle over his knee again, security camera be damned. A scab had formed on his knee where he'd cut it open on the far side of the River Styx. Martin ran his finger gently over the rough souvenir of his recent adventures. He closed his eyes and let his experiences in the afterlife finally overwhelm him.

This, he thought, must be why they favor waiting rooms so much on the other side, to give souls the chance to reflect on things before they head back into the fray. What was that old quote about the unexamined life? Martin decided he would use his waiting time to thoroughly and completely examine his so that when he found himself in the next one, he could do everything right, make as few mistakes as possible.

"Fartin? Fartin Van AssMan?"

Martin opened his eyes and sat up straight. A thin man wearing wire-rimmed glasses, a dark jacket, and a tie was standing in the doorway looking at him. He seemed a little nervous.

"It's Martin," Martin said, getting to his feet. "Martin with an M. Martin Van Assen. It's Dutch."

The man frowned down at some paperwork in his hand. "Sorry," he said. "I'm still kind of new here. Is this you?" he asked. He held out a form for Martin to inspect. Martin recognized it as his own from the pile the receptionist had handed him. At the top, though, someone had crossed out his real name and written his afterlife friends' annoying nickname for him in its place.

"Yeah," Martin said, laughing. "That's me."

The man pulled a pen out of an inside jacket pocket and corrected the error. "Sorry," he said, sounding irritated. "The angels just brought us a new guy to work in the back office and he seems to have a juvenile sense of humor."

Martin's eyes got wide. "Zeke?" he asked. "Is his name Zeke Zabar?"

"Yeah," the man holding Martin's paperwork said. "They rescued him from one of Satan's torture chambers or something. You know him?"

"Yeah," Martin said with a smile. "We go way back."

The man put away his pen, looked at Martin's corrected paperwork, then looked back at Martin again. "Alright, Mr. Van Assen," he said. "It's time to go."

And, with a deep breath, Martin went.

A.L. Glennon

Acknowlededgments

I am grateful for all the help and support I have received while waiting to see *Wait for It* come into the world.

Thank you to my friends and family for all of your encouragement, especially my parents who taught me to love words.

Thanks to my beta readers, Tabitha and Anna. I know how busy you both are and I am very grateful that you made time to go through my manuscript.

I also owe a huge debt of gratitude to all the Wordsmiths, past and present, for believing me when I showed up at a meeting and said I was a writer! Special thanks to our fearless leader, Darcey, to Flurrin, for always knowing what I'm trying to say even when I choose the wrong words, and to Geoff for the extra time he dedicated to this manuscript as well as all his moral support.

A mere thank you doesn't seem like enough for my husband, Jason, who's always my first reader and who never stops encouraging me to follow my dreams. I love you. Thank you, too, to Sebastian, Reese, and Caden for being my biggest cheerleaders and constantly reminding me that books are the best! I love you guys, too!

Finally, a heartfelt thank you goes out to every reader who has followed Martin, Zeke, and Zelda on their journey. I am truly honored that you did so.

Meet A.L. Glennon

A.L. Glennon has a Master of Arts degree from the Communication, Culture, and Technology Program at Georgetown University. She currently lives in North Carolina with her husband and three sons.